**Eric Ambler** was born into a family of entertainers and in his early years helped out as a puppeteer. However, he initially chose engineering as a full time career, although this quickly gave way to writing. In World War II he entered the army and looked likely to fight in the line, but was soon after commissioned and ended the war as assistant director of the army film unit and a Lieutenant-Colonel.

This experience translated into civilian life and Ambler had a very successful career as a screen writer, receiving an Academy Award for his work on *The Cruel Sea* by Nicolas Monsarrat in 1953. Many of his own works have been filmed, the most famous probably being *Light of Day*, filmed as *Topkapi* under which title it is now published.

He established a reputation as a thriller writer of extraordinary depth and originality and received many other accolades during his lifetime, including two *Edgar Awards* from *The Mystery Writers of America* (best novel for *Topkapi* and best biographical work for *Here Lies Eric Ambler)*, and two *Gold Dagger Awards* from the *Crime Writer's Association (Passage of Arms* and *The Levanter)*.

Often credited as being the inventor of the modern political thriller, *John Le Carre* once described Ambler as '*the source on which we all draw.*' A recurring theme in his works is the success of the well meaning yet somewhat bungling amateur who triumphs in the face of both adversity and hardened professionals.

Ambler wrote under his own name and also during the 1950's a series of novels as *Eliot Reed*, with *Charles Rhodda*. These are now published under the '*Ambler*' umbrella.

Works of **ERIC AMBLER** published by
**HOUSE OF STRATUS**

DOCTOR FRIGO
JUDGMENT ON DELTCHEV
THE LEVANTER
THE SCHIRMER INHERITANCE
THE SIEGE OF THE VILLA LIPP (Also as 'Send No More Roses')
TOPKAPI (Also as 'The Light Of Day')

**Originally as Eliot Reed with Charles Rhodda:**
CHARTER TO DANGER
THE MARAS AFFAIR
PASSPORT TO PANIC
TENDER TO DANGER (Also as 'Tender To Moonlight')
SKYTIP

**Autobiography:**
HERE LIES ERIC AMBLER

# The Maras Affair

*eric Ambler*

This edition published in 2009 by House of Stratus, an imprint of
Stratus Books Ltd., 21 Beeching Park, Kelly Bray,
Cornwall, PL17 8QS, UK.

www.houseofstratus.com

A catalogue record for this book is available from the British Library and the Library of Congress.

ISBN 0-7551-1764-6
EAN 978-0-7551-1764-2

# I

Sokolny came into the office quite excited about a new scheme for an escape across the frontier. He extolled it like a carpet salesman. It would be a big story; something to make a sensation. No, it was not merely the seizure of another aeroplane. That, as everyone knew, was becoming difficult as well as hackneyed. As for those poor dolts who gambled against the mines between the zones of barbed wire, the statistics alone were enough! Not two in ten got through. Perhaps not one in ten. Nowadays, the job needed daring, imagination, careful preparation. No wonder the price was going up. It took all of fifteen hundred dollars to get you out of the country today. Now, this story he was hoping to get would show that . . .

Burton listened without interest. At that time it was nothing that concerned him personally, nor could he see that it would ever concern him. If it came off, it would be just another news story for the censor to kill. The sensation, if any, would be worked up by some news man beyond the corridor of mines and watchtowers.

He interrupted Sokolny. "You'd better go along to the Trade Ministry. There's a statement to pick up. Give it to Anna if I'm not in."

Sokolny shrugged. Burton was a little worried. He didn't like Sokolny and his confidential reports. They were dangerous; especially to the man himself. Unless, of course, he invented them to justify the continuance of his retainer. It was also possible that he was simply a spy, put in by the regime to test and report on the doings of the *Star-Dispatch* office. Foreign correspondents were always suspect; Americans, possibly, more than others.

Burton saw the door of the outer office close slowly behind Sokolny. He walked to the window and looked out. The prospect was one of fine streets, of noble buildings, and pleasant gardens, but what he saw with his mind's eye was a pattern of intrigue and fear, of treachery, and of shifting loyalties that formed and broke up and formed again beneath the surface of imposed order.

More than ever Sokolny seemed part of the pattern. A nervous, irresolute man with big dark eyes in a pale wedge of a face who could never stand long on two feet, but was always shifting his weight from one foot to the other. There was not much weight to shift. The worn suit flapped on his thin frame; the collar of his shirt seemed always a size too large.

Burton had wanted to get rid of him at the start, but his predecessor had advised strongly against it. "Sokolny's useful. I've got him well trained. More important, you can trust him. You'll learn what that means before you're much older. Unless you're just going to sit back and take the official handouts, you're going to have plenty of trouble coming."

Not an entirely reliable witness, Don Glover; and not, perhaps, a very good judge of men like Stephan Sokolny. Don had got himself in trouble in no time, and the *Star-Dispatch* had been forced to haul him out. But part of his testimony had been sound; Burton had soon been up against the trouble.

There were long arguments with the censorship about fatuous details. Every kind of obstruction was put in his way. The officials were pleasant people, most affable. They laughed. They told you funny stories even while they killed your copy. They were always so reasonable, so regretful, so sensible of the dignity of the *Star-Dispatch*, so sensitive to the opinion of New York. They were appreciative, too, of Mr. Burton, realising that he understood all the difficulties. Unfortunately his colleague, Mr. Glover, had not always exercised the patience that was sometimes necessary. They were sure Mr. Burton would be different.

After one especially fantastic series of conferences, he had written to New York that he was wasting his time and their money; but nothing had come of it. Spring had arrived and the Dreva had continued to flow under the ten bridges.

At the end of May the political police arrested Frank Murch and sent him back to his Chicago editor with love and kisses. Burton had tried vainly to get a cable through about it. Then he had told New York that he wanted a transfer, he was tired of being an office boy. They had urged him to be patient until another job became available.

Months later, when they offered him Vienna, he had turned it down.

"I'd better stay on," he said.

He sighed. Perhaps the sluggish Dreva had got into his blood. Or was it that he liked the view of St. Trophimus from the office window, the oxide green of the onion domes against the high blue of the November sky? He smiled grimly at this unlikely notion, turned from the window, and glanced through the doorway into the outer office, where Anna Maras was dealing with the foreign language newspapers.

She could read anything, from Greek to Episcopal Slavonic, and at first he had praised her talent, her intelligence, and her industry. Now he saw more in the colour of her hair, but tried to deny to himself that this was important. More vehemently he tried to deny that he was hanging on to the job because of Anna Maras. He assured himself that the reason was very different. It was the newspaper man's sense of something impending, and it had grown on him more and more throughout the summer. If he worried about Anna Maras, it was because he felt responsible for her in a vague way. A thought would come nagging about the girl who had worked for Frank Murch. What had happened to her? A reward? A punishment? All he knew was that she had dropped out of sight, and, in the international hullabaloo over Murch's deportation, no one had bothered to inquire about her.

Appointments had to be vetted, of course, and no doubt these girls were loyal servants of the regime. If they accepted an invitation to dine or to go to the opera or ballet with you in their spare time, it was probably with the approval of the responsible bureau. One had to be thankful that the responsible bureau had the good taste to pick someone as lovely as Anna.

Thankful for one so disturbing?

Burton scowled at his desk. There had been an incident; a playful embrace in parting one night after one of those social occasions. At least he had intended it to be playful. It was in a light mood of laughter, a gesture of affection, but, at the moment of touch, there was a lightning-swift change in the girl. She drew back startled, then reached towards him and held him.

Disconcerting? Yet he knew at the moment that this was what he wanted, and he felt it with the more intensity because he was not the habitual hunter. Disconcerting? He was surprised, perhaps, by the frankness of this affirmation or avowal or whatever it was, but he was glad of it.

On the way back to his hotel he thought bitterly that this sort of thing was possibly within her brief; she would have him tied up, just where she wanted him. Then he condemned himself for the unworthy thought. He had learned little about her in the months she had worked for him, but he had the conviction that she was at least emotionally honest. He sometimes put it to himself that she was quite genuine, quite sincere; that she would not betray him, whatever her briefing. But, then, there was never going to be anything to betray. One thing he had determined from the beginning: he was not going to get mixed up in anything political. This was even more necessary, since he had committed himself to Anna.

But Anna, the next morning, had given no sign that he had committed himself to anything. Her behaviour had been fastidiously correct, and so it had continued in the days that followed. Away from the office she might relax a little, but at the first sign of an advance from him she would retreat. She believed, perhaps, that the situation was hopeless; that there could be no serious development of their relationship. He might be moved on to another country at any time, and in no circumstances would she be permitted to accompany him. Not legally. Not without grave risk. So she was making it easy for him to be wise, but he was not always enamoured of wisdom. There was something bleak about it, and this day, as he stood in his office scowling at his desk, he felt the bleakness acutely.

The phone bell rang, drawing his glance back to the outer office. He had a glimpse of the girl's fine profile in the afternoon sunlight when she turned to reach for the receiver.

She spoke a few sentences and her voice became tense. It was still tense when she called him.

"For you," she said. "The Police Judiciary."

"Mr. Charles Burton?" The official at the Judiciary was very polite. It was desired that Mr. Burton should attend at a particular office; a mere formality connected with the representation of the *Star-Dispatch*. If Mr. Burton would name an agreeable hour, every endeavour would be made to meet his convenience.

Burton said, "I'll come right away. Will that be agreeable?"

When he put the receiver down Anna Maras was standing beside him, her face marked by anxiety. "What is it?" she demanded.

"What should it be?" He laughed. "We've skipped some tax or missed a form we should have filled in."

"Whom must you see?"

"Fellow named Sesnik. Know him?"

"Yes."

He heard fear in her voice.

"Look, Anna, what is this? What have you got to be frightened about?"

"Nothing." She turned away, hesitated, came back. "If it's about Pero Trovic, please be careful. Say nothing of Sokolny."

"What do you know of Pero Trovic?"

Something made it hard for her to speak. She started, and then checked herself.

"I know," she said at last; but that was all she said.

# II

Sesnik reached across the wide top of his desk with a photograph in his podgy hand. It was a bromide repro of a pensive young man, chin resting on hand, forefinger laid along a lean cheek. An amateur poet with money, or the juvenile lead in a comedy by Turgenev. An inescapable suggestion of ham in the pose swung the odds in favour of the actor. He was handsome. He had a good brow, a fine straight nose, full lips, lively eyes. He conveyed an impression of youthful ease and comfortable living. His confidence amounted to smugness. He was aware of his barbered smoothness and the very effective cut of his clothes.

"You know him?" Sesnik asked hopefully. "You are not sure, perhaps? Take it in your hand, please. Look again."

Burton squinted, half closing his eyes. Then he had it. The actor took on a new make-up. The face became strained and lined and the hair was an untrimmed mass. Instead of smugness, the eyes had a hunted look. It was suspicion in them, rather than fear, and they showed the weariness that comes from being constantly on the alert. Burton had seen that weariness many times up and down Europe since the war. But he had seen something more in the eyes of this changed young man: desperation, courage, determination. He did not know how to describe it. It confirmed Sokolny's furtive testimonial. "A good man. He will do the job. Mr. Glover sometimes used him."

Sesnik had the reedy voice of a persuasive bassoon. "The

photograph is six years old perhaps. He has since grown a moustache. A little moustache."

"Yes, of course," Burton agreed. "His name is Pero Trovic."

His nonchalance must have been convincing enough, but Sesnik stared at him as if he wanted to hypnotise him into some betrayal.

"He does a bit of work for us now and then," Burton added. "I don't know much about him. Haven't been here long enough. Surely he's not in any trouble?"

Behind his mask of impassivity he was wondering how Anna Maras had been able to divine the purpose of Sesnik's summons.

The official shifted his corpulent body within the tight compass of a revolving armchair.

"He does a bit of work for you," he repeated speculatively. "Now and then?" The round moonface with the small eyes, button nose, and the gentle comical mouth came nearer as he leaned over the blotter. "Eight days ago he applied to the Propaganda Ministry for a permit to visit the village of Kazyos. The application had your endorsement."

"Sure. There's nothing wrong with that. It was suggested that he get a story on the resumption of the Horse Fair."

"This is very flattering." Sesnik's smile suggested a great breadth of geniality. "The New York *Star-Dispatch* is interested in the disposal of ten spavined cart horses in a squalid mountain village?"

Burton protested that Mr. Sesnik was being a little too modest. The Fair at Kazyos was traditional, famed in song and story. The muster of horses might not be so large in present circumstances, but the social gathering was important. The colour, the customs, the history of it would make an article for the Sunday magazine section. The Propaganda Ministry had undertaken to supply pictures.

Sesnik found it all very funny. "The peasant girls in their finery, the visiting gypsies with their fiddles and concertinas. And the ten sad horses! Who suggested this journalistic enterprise? Was it Trovic himself?"

"Yes, it was."

"So!"

"What's wrong with it?" Burton put a little bite into the question. "We look to our local helpers to make suggestions of that sort."

"Or the great world would never hear of Kazyos and its Horse Fair." Sesnik found it convulsing, but suddenly shed his laughter. "Are you aware how far Kazyos is from the frontier?"

"I don't see what that has to do with it."

"You travelled people never know your geography. Have you received your story from Trovic?"

Burton made a gesture of impatience. "The fair began yesterday. I don't expect anything till next week."

Sesnik's moonface was solemn as he shook his head slowly. "If you did not expect anything till next year, you would still be disappointed."

"Are you suggesting that there is no fair at Kazyos?"

"The fair, my dear sir, opened yesterday according to schedule. I am merely suggesting that Kazyos is quite close to the frontier. Trovic crossed it two days ago. He was, perhaps, a good news gatherer. He must have learned a lot in a short time about the mined area and the barbed wire. He was shot at and wounded, but he reached the British zone. I do not question your good faith, Mr. Burton, but I have to impress it upon you that a dangerous criminal has made use of you. If he had attempted to get a rail ticket through any office less doltish than the Propaganda Ministry, I would have been informed in time."

Burton frowned. His position was not a comfortable one, but he came back at Sesnik.

"If you're right about Trovic, why wasn't I informed about him in time? You must have known he was on our books."

"Regard me, please, Mr. Burton." Sesnik's appeal had an almost boyish candour. "I am a man, like yourself. Perhaps I have not the astuteness of an American correspondent. I learn more and more as the days pass, but omniscience is beyond me." He picked up the bromide repro from the desk. "This handsome young man once acted at our National Theatre under the name of Andreas Nimsky. Pero Trovic is, perhaps, just another of his roles. How often, since your arrival among us, have you used him on your newspaper assignments?"

"This was the first time."

"Indeed!" If one so round as Mr. Sesnik could have sat bolt upright, he would have achieved it then. His head smacked the back of the chair. "I understood you to say that this Trovic was a regular contributor."

"Now and then," Burton corrected him. "I merely took him over from my colleague, Don Glover."

"Ah, yes. Mr. Glover. I knew him quite well before he departed."

"You probably attended his departure." Burton was getting annoyed.

"By proxy." Sesnik produced one of his disarming smiles. '"The complaint came from another ministry. But, please, we will return to Trovic. How frequently did Mr. Glover employ him?"

"I can't tell you offhand. I'll have to look it up."

"No doubt Mr. Glover recommended him to you?"

"I can't recollect."

"Did anyone recommend him?"

He remembered Anna's anxious injunction. "Please be careful. Say nothing of Sokolny."

They'd used Sokolny and Anna Maras. They had involved him in a plot to get this Trovic out of the country. It was improbable that Trovic had ever been in the office before the day Sokolny brought him in.

"Why do you hesitate?" Sesnik inquired helpfully.

"I'm not hesitating." Burton could hear his own voice getting harder. "No one recommended him. I'm telling you I took him over, like the files and the chairs and the typewriters."

"And Sokolny," Sesnik added. "A satisfactory man, I believe, Sokolny?"

"Very satisfactory."

"And Miss Prazatto?"

"Miss Prazatto was not available after Glover's departure. Surely you remember that?"

"Of course, of course. I grow so forgetful. You now have Miss Maras. A charming girl. Brilliant career at our university, such as it is. I have a deep regard for Anna. Socially, I mean. I might claim to have helped her a little. I knew her mother. A witty Frenchwoman. Charming. There are associations with your country, by the way. One of Anna's aunts married into a Boston family. You must ask the girl some time. She's very interested in America. Between you and me, she always wanted a job with an American newspaper. That's where I stepped in. Her name was given a good position on the panel. I should have remembered, of course." Remembered what?"

"That she had been allocated to your office. You understand, don't you, that this has nothing to do officially with the Police Judiciary?"

"I understand that the usual procedure was followed."

"But my part in it was purely personal, as a friend of the family."

"You don't have to apologise, Mr. Sesnik."

"Apologise?" Sesnik was puzzled. "Ah, I see what you mean." His body quaked flabbily as he laughed. "In any case, Mr. Burton, if the girl gives you trouble, you will know where to bring your complaints."

"There aren't likely to be any."

"I'm glad to hear it." Sesnik hauled himself up from his chair and waddled round the great desk, balancing precariously on small feet in glinting black shoes. "I want to see her get on. Her ambition is to translate books from the American and the English." He reached up with a fat caressing hand as Burton rose. "Well, my dear sir, I am most happy to know you. If you wish for anything, I shall always be at your service. Meanwhile, look up the assignments your colleague gave to Trovic, will you? Make out a little list." Sesnik brought his heavy forefinger to within an inch of his thumb. "Just a little list."

# III

Anna Maras had gone for the day. It was still early, but there was no hard-and-fast timing in the office. Sometimes she worked late. If she had little to do, she might leave any time after four. It was a fact, though, that she usually waited in if Burton was out, and now he wondered if she had gone early to evade any questions he might bring back from the Police Judiciary. She had left a note on his desk.

"Sokolny has gone home. He was feeling bad with his teeth. I have taken the trade report with me. Here is digest of an important item. Nothing else. I wish to see Babette, so have gone early. A.M."

It was feasible. Her friend Babette, subject to the stern regimen of the ballet dancer, would have to be early at the Opera House.

He looked at the important item and decided that it wasn't worth cabling. He took down the book in which outside assignments were recorded for expense-account purposes. He had a feeling that there would be no list to make out for Mr. Sesnik, but that was not why he left the book unopened on his desk. He had remembered suddenly that the usual night for the ballet was Wednesday, and this was Tuesday. He went to the front office to find the week's bill.

They were doing Sadko.

That was all right then. They'd be using the dancers. What was not all right was this tendency in him to get too suspicious.

He stood staring at the opera bill, reading it without purpose, without apprehension. Wednesday: Swan Lake, Vera Kurtz . . .

The telephone rang.

It was Sokolny.

"Please, Mr. Burton, the dentist has agreed to see me in the morning."

"All right. Get in as soon as you can. I want to talk to you."

He frowned impatiently. He had spoken far too sharply. His suspicions of Sokolny were not yet justified. The man's teeth were terrible. He had been suffering for weeks.

Burton went back to his desk and opened the assignment book at a page that bore entries in Glover's untidy scrawl. The first name he saw was Trovic's. So Sesnik would have his little list after all.

Trovic was the only casual hand that Glover had used. He had given jobs to Sokolny, and Sophie Prazatto had covered two or three things on the feminine side. Over a period of two years, the full period of Glover's tour of duty in this Utopia, Trovic had been paid for six articles, all of them on village or pastoral subjects.

Burton felt better as he scribbled the details on a sheet of copy paper. The suggestion that he had been made use of was out. The *Star-Dispatch* could not be held responsible for the aberration of an irregular contributor. Anyone might be seized suddenly with the desire to skip across the frontier. Even Mr. Sesnik.

The picture of that bulbous body waddling among the trip wires in highly polished shoes was too much. It had to end in an explosion. Mr. Sesnik went out like a pricked balloon. Burton laughed. When he had finished for the day, he left the little list in the outer office for Anna Maras to type.

Next morning a batch of American mail kept him cheerfully busy, and it was not until the girl brought him the list that he gave another thought to the Trovic affair. It was tiresome, but quite unimportant. He grinned, recalling again the comical figure of Mr. Sesnik. The girl's eyes were grave.

"What did he have to say to you?" she asked.

"Only that you have an aunt in Boston," Burton answered. "You didn't tell me he was a friend of the family."

"I beg you not to make such jokes. Please tell me what he said about Trovic."

"He won't be doing any more work for us."

She jerked back as if from a sudden pain and he stared at her coldly.

"He's not dead, if that's what you're worried about," he said. "He's safe. Out of it. He got across the frontier near Kazyos. He didn't wait to cover the Horse Fair."

It took her a while to grasp this information. She stared at him, her pale face going paler. He saw bewilderment in her eyes and something that looked like disbelief.

"No." The tone was sharp now. "It can't be true. He would never----" She pulled herself up sharply and turned from him to face the window.

"Sesnik believes it," he told her. "He seems to think we may have had a hand in it. *That* isn't true, is it?"

"You know it isn't." Her shoulders lifted slightly.

"The implication is that we helped him by sending him to Kazyos."

"How could Sesnik think that?" She continued to face the window, looking out on the boulevards and the green domes of St. Trophimus.

"I might, of course, be a first-class sucker," Burton answered her; "another of the innocent, ingenuous American fools. Too simple and trusting. Sokolny, for instance. I've trusted him quite a bit, haven't I?"

"Sokolny is the fool, if there is a fool."

"So you think Sokolny worked it?"

"I don't think." The answer was just audible. She added, raising her voice, "You have the previous assignments to show Sesnik. What can he do to you?"

"Nothing. I'm not worried." He got up and went to her. "I want to know why you asked me to keep Sokolny out of it."

"Because he's so helpless. It's not good to get him involved in anything."

"Then you knew that something was going on?" He waited. "Answer me, Anna!"

"I knew that Trovic was in trouble."

"And you didn't think it necessary to warn me?"

"Please." She turned to him and he saw her anxious eyes. "I wasn't here when Sokolny brought him in. I did not know him by the name of Trovic. Afterwards I heard who he was."

"Andreas Nimsky?" "Andreas . . ." She was surprised or puzzled. She gazed at him, and then turned to the window once more. "All right," she agreed. "Andreas Nimsky. One name is as good as another. He worked for you as Trovic. That was one of his lives."

"Has he got many?"

"We have come through hard times." She kept her face resolutely towards the window. She spoke slowly, choosing her words carefully. "Sometimes some of us have been uncertain. There have been changes. The wind shifts, and you have to have courage to stand against it."

"Do you stand against it?"

"I am not speaking of myself."

"I want to know," he insisted.

"I love my country. I am your servant. If you think I am not loyal to you, you must let me go." She turned from him and walked quickly into the outer office, pulling the door to behind her.

He moved to the window and looked down the street towards the river. A crowd swarmed at one end of the Alexis Bridge, opposite the tall Radio Building. Two cars were in a jam and a policeman was in violent altercation with the drivers. The scene was so normal, so ordinary; it might have been in New York or any other American city, except for the background.

The policeman waved his arms decisively, the cars backed out of the clinch, the crowd melted away.

Burton was still standing at the window when the girl returned from the outer office.

"I'm sorry," she said. "I was not polite."

"Forget it," he told her. "You don't have to apologise."

"Here is the report from the Trade Ministry. I don't think you'll find much in it for New York."

There was a new reserve in her, a distance between them. She wanted to be the correct servant, to deny any human relationship. He smiled as she went towards the door again. At the last moment he stopped her.

"By the way, did you see your friend Babette last night?"

"Yes." She halted, her hand on the door.

"How is she getting on?"

"Very well, thank you. She is dancing the Swan *Lake* tonight."

"Yes. I saw the bill. Vera Kurtz, isn't it?"

"No. It is Babette. Vera Kurtz has hurt a knee and Radkina is ill. It is Babette's chance."

Excitement over her friend's good fortune broke down her solemnity. It was something. It was a miracle. The fledgling, the pretty cygnet, would take the wings and the crown of the Swan Princess.

"The news came last night. It was posted on the board before she reached the theatre. Velic was standing in the doorway. He embraced her, and that was the first she knew of it. 'Hail to Odette,' he said. 'Welcome Odile. I salute our new ballerina.' "

"Well, you'll want to get off early, won't you?"

"Thank you. You are considerate." She was his servant again, and the sparkle left her eyes. "A friend is trying to get me a seat, but it is difficult. If I leave early, I can make up for it tomorrow."

"Yes, you can do that."

This time her gravity was not so amusing. It disturbed him. She went to her job of combing the local newspapers for items. Burton closed the door and telephoned an official at the Propaganda Ministry for ballet tickets.

"Tonight, I regret, it is impossible," the official said. "The house is sold out for Kurtz, though she will not be dancing. You should have given me a few days' notice, Mr. Burton."

Burton argued. The theatre administration must have some seats in reserve, or there might be some returns. The official had further regrets. Under the method of distribution there was little likelihood of returns. Swan *Lake,* with or without Kurtz, was very popular. Mr. Burton could be assured of seats for the next performance by Kurtz. In any case, the new ballerina, Trepleva, would not interest him. She was of no international significance.

"You're supposed to look after the foreign press, aren't you?" Burton retorted. "My paper is interested in Trepleva. Kurtz couldn't make the news if she danced the cancan on a slack wire. Just try the theatre and call me back."

He tackled his American mail, but could not concentrate. He was impatient with himself and guilty. Burton the boor! It was inexcusable to pour crude scorn on a national idol like Vera Kurtz simply because the press liaison office could not supply him with tickets to see another dancer. And why did he have to be so deeply concerned about whether or not Anna Maras saw her friend make her debut as a ballerina?

The official at the Propaganda Ministry called back about midday. He had tried every possible source, he said, but not a seat was to be had in the house. Burton thanked him, too warmly, for trying.

# IV

When he returned from lunch it was late in the afternoon. Anna motioned towards the closed door of his room and shaped two syllables with her lips. He heard no sound, but he could read the name.

Sesnik.

She had been nursing her alarm and it showed plainly as she moved forward to meet him. She whispered, "He came a half hour ago and insisted on waiting in your room. I didn't know where to reach you." "It's all right," Burton assured her. "I should have sent him the Trovic list. I forgot about it. Don't worry."

"There is something else."

"What?"

"A messenger brought the article on the Kazyos fair."

"What!" His voice rose involuntarily. "Trovic's article?"

"It's typewritten. No signature. It must have been sent from Kazyos yesterday. There is a note to say that the payment is covered by the expenses advance."

"These amateurs! Give me the article."

"It is not yet translated."

"Get it for me!"

She glanced with increased apprehension towards the closed door. "That man must not know."

"We'll see."

She brought him a thin fold of quarto sheets. He glanced at the article, but could understand only a sprinkling of the more familiar words he had picked up. It had been done on an old and decrepit machine with a rock-hard platen and worn type abominably out of alignment. He thrust the sheets into the breast pocket of his jacket and opened the door of his room.

Sesnik turned from the window, swivelling awkwardly on the soles of his radiant shoes.

"I congratulate you on your view, Mr. Burton," he said. "Were I an artist, I would wish to paint the ten bridges from this very spot. I have been admiring the perpendicular of our own Judiciary building. It is rarely that we get far enough away from the trees to appreciate the wood. We are a city of many styles, but they are reconciled, I think, in a beautiful synthesis."

"I'll take your word for it. I don't know much about architectural synthesis."

"Possibly you do yourself an injustice." Sesnik laughed as if he had said something irresistibly funny. "I hope you will for-give this intrusion. I was passing your doorway and I thought I would step in. I have been talking to Anna; keeping her from her work, I fear. She is so like her French mother, with her blue eyes and her light gold hair. Fortunately there is little of that dull creature Maras in her. I find her very intelligent, but she seems a little pale today. I hope you are not working her too hard."

"I don't think so." Burton was being patient but stiff. "I suppose you've come about the Trovic assignments? Here is the list."

He found the sheet on his desk and handed it over. Sesnik examined it carefully; seemed to read it twice, and then a third time. He frowned. He teetered precariously on his polished shoes, till Burton, fearful for his balance, requested him to sit down.

Still focussing on the list, he squeezed himself into the chair at the side of the desk.

"This is very interesting," he commented, and the small eyes in the moonface gazed probingly at Burton. "Very interesting indeed. I wonder if you realise, my dear friend, what you have placed in my hands. It is a ray, a searching ray. It throws a new light upon certain events and links them in series. It opens up an exciting line for investigation. Very exciting."

Burton's blank face masked his concern. "I'm afraid I don't know what you're talking about."

"I will show you. A sheet of paper, if you please." Sesnik's podgy finger uncapped a fountain pen. He reached for the sheet of paper and drew an indented line upon it with a nice precision. "Perhaps the details are not exact," he said, "but this is intended to be our western frontier, from the Carpathians to the Dreva. Now here is Kazyos." He placed a dot near one of the indentations, and then added other dots to the map, naming them as he did so. "Murnitz, Kars, Jyssic, Trodz, Kleebach, Prebl. Each place, you see, is quite close to the frontier, and each place has been the scene, the background, so to speak, of an escape."

"What about it?"

"Each place has also been the background of a little journalistic excursion for Trovic."

"A remarkable coincidence!" Burton stared at the map, too taken aback to realise the inanity of his own words.

"A remarkable series of coincidences," Sesnik amended. "Even more remarkable if our escape dates coincide with the travels of Trovic. I will check. But I have no doubt that he has been behind these criminal escapes, like that character of the English books, the *Scarlet* . . . what is it?"

*"Pimpernel."*

"But nothing so romantic. You see now, my friend, how your office has been used to aid the flight of lawbreakers and assassins. I don't blame you that you have been taken in by this scheming malefactor, but I blame your Mr. Glover for carelessness. Perhaps he did not stop at carelessness."

"Wait a minute, Mr. Sesnik." Burton's lips tightened angrily. "I'm not going to listen to any charges against Glover or anybody else on the staff of my paper. You can theorise about Trovic as much as you like. . . ."

"I can theorise." Sesnik's small eyes sparked as he cut in. "I can theorise that Glover was taken in repeatedly by suggestions from Trovic, suggestions that he should go to Murnitz, to Kars, to Trodz. By the way, you have a man named Sokolny on your staff. I would like to meet him."

"Sokolny is little more than a messenger. He looks after the office. He is not important."

"It is an axiom of the Judiciary that the unimportant have eyes and ears like the important. You know there is a serious charge upon us, Mr. Burton. We are responsible for the security of the State, the heads of the State, our distinguished visitors. We are responsible for you and Anna Maras and Sokolny. I would like to talk to Sokolny."

"He hasn't appeared today. I think he's having some teeth out."

"Please let me have his address."

"I'm sure he can't give you any help," he said. "Anyway, your Trovic has bolted, so what's the use?"

"My dear friend, do you think there is only Trovic in this business? There is an organization, a gang that attracts all the criminals of the underworld, the reactionary counter-revolutionaries, the political assassins, and saboteurs. Do you think my work is ever done? My dear friend!"

Sesnik wrenched himself from the arms of the chair and got to his feet with grunting noises. "You need have no fear that I will be harsh with Sokolny. I have suffered from teeth myself." He fumbled in his breast pocket, produced a wallet with difficulty, and then searched its various divisions with a thick forefinger. Burton, rising to escort him to the door, watched him curiously.

"It occurs to me," Sesnik went on, "that you may be interested in the ballet. It is quite one of our most promising cultural institutions. Not comparable, of course, to Moscow or Leningrad, but the best, I daresay, among the newer of the free democracies. I had tickets . . . ah, yes, here they are. Will you please accept them with my compliments? For tonight, I'm afraid. I'm sorry the notice is so short. If you are unable to use them, perhaps you have a friend."

Another coincidence?

Burton stared. Nothing could be more innocent of guile than the moonface of Mr. Sesnik.

"You mustn't deprive yourself."

But the generous man had already deprived himself. The tickets were on the desk and Mr. Sesnik was waddling from the room." Please, no inconvenience," he begged. "I will say a little word or two to Anna on my way out."

An avuncular farewell, no doubt. In a moment the outer door was closed. Sesnik had departed. Burton took the Kazyos story from his pocket, put a match to it, carried the blazing sheets to the grate, and then stooped to break up the ashes with a poker. When he turned, Anna Maras was standing in the doorway, watching him.

She said, "Sokolny came in. He was frightened when I told him who was with you. He ran away. He said he would wait in the café across the road. He told me the dentist would do nothing for him till next week. I don't believe he went to the man."

"You look scared yourself." Burton was studying her closely. "We've nothing to fear from Sesnik. What is it?"

"Sokolny." Her gaze fell away from his. "I don't trust him."

"If he were a police spy, why should he run away from Sesnik?"

"It's not that." Her hands moved in a gesture of denial.

"You think he was mixed up with Trovic. That's why you asked me to keep him out of it."

"I don't know. You must believe me, I don't know. I'm afraid of what might happen if Sesnik gets hold of him. Sokolny will talk. He will say anything. He has no courage."

"You're anxious for Trovic's friends, is that it?"

She hesitated. "I am anxious for all my friends, for any who may be involved. I have no knowledge, but I may suspect. Do you understand? There are times when a man keeps his acts secret from his brother. If I had a brother I might fear for him, without having knowledge."

"Or without cause?"

"That is how it is." She closed her eyes for a moment, and then met his gaze frankly. "I have put myself in your hands."

At that moment he was suspicious of her, but he did not allow the fact to show in his face. He said, "I know no more of you than I ever did. I'm not interested in anyone's politics except when they make news."

"You encourage Sokolny in dangerous work. He brings you tales and rumours. Yesterday he brought you the tale of an escape plan."

"That's what I employ him for. His tales are safe enough with me."

"But they are not safe with him. Perhaps he blunders on these things. I don't know. He is a mindless scavenger. He is like the simpleton in *Boris,* who looks in the snow for a lost kopeck. One day he will find more than a kopeck."

"In plain words, without the operatic allusions, a stick of dynamite."

"I don't think you should laugh at me. Perhaps he has already found the kopeck."

"I'm beginning to think that I've found it. Maybe I'm not wasting my time after all." Burton laughed. "Go home and put on your Sunday best. I've two seats for the ballet."

She was still solemn, refusing to meet his change of mood. "I've already arranged," she said. "I will find somewhere to stand."

He picked up the tickets and glanced at them. "First tier," he remarked. "They'll be giving us the State Box next. Do you want to waste such a chance to see your friend? Come! We'll send a big bouquet of red roses. From Anna and her boss. You run off home. I'll go to the flower shop."

She agreed, but with no enthusiasm. "There's plenty of time," she said. "First I'll do some work on the article from Kazyos, if you will let me have it."

"No," he answered. "That's out. We're not going to use it."

She looked at the ashes in the fireplace. "You are very good," she said.

"Me, good!" He was uneasy. It was a reproach. He preferred to apply epithets of a different sort to himself. He was tough, cunning, ruthless, hardhearted, even mean, but never good. He would sell his grandmother for a ten-line beat; his best friend for an exclusive picture. Sometimes, he even believed it; though he had no grandmother. Good? He must be getting senile.

"You think I'd send that stuff along to the censor?" he demanded irritably. "They've got a private line to the Police Judiciary. What would Sesnik think? Do you want to upset the man?"

Once more the frightened look came to her eyes.

"So it is Trovic," he said.

She did not deny it. She said, "I'm very tired. I want to go away."

"Where do you want to go?"

"Out of it! Out of it altogether!"

He sighed. It was possible, of course, to buy a passage to America, but the preliminary stages of the journey were apt to be irksome. Running the Dreva in a canoe was about as safe as going over Niagara in a barrel. And the alternative . . . ?

Sesnik's crude map of the frontier was still on the desk.

"Perhaps he'll arrange it somehow." Burton was not hopeful. He had to say something in an attempt to comfort her. "He'll send for you?"

"Who will?"

"Trovic. I don't believe he'll desert you. He'd be a fool."

She looked up quickly, their eyes meeting, he had a desire to take hold of her.

"You don't understand at all," she said. "I'm frightened of what may happen, and there's nothing I can do."

"You'd better go home and change, hadn't you?" he said.

## V

He watched her in the glow from the great stage. He had no eyes for the cavortings of the village maidens and the young nobles from the castle. The music of Tchaikovsky seemed dull and distant and sometimes it did not reach him at all. The Prince's entry meant nothing. He was absorbed in the girl beside him, finding an unfamiliar beauty in the sweep of her hair from her brow, in the fine lines of her profile, the slightly parted lips. He could also sense the tension in her.

She had been in a highly nervous state when she had arrived, and there had been more to it than the fact that she had been late and breathless from running. She had gained control of herself now, but it was a very tight control. She could not have been more nervous had she been cast as the Odette of this *Swan Lake*, an Odette who had never worn a tutu or achieved a single fouette.

The house lights had already been dimmed down when they took their seats, and her few words of apology for having kept him waiting were drowned by the applause for the conductor. She said something about a traffic mishap, but Burton was too relieved by her arrival to pay any attention. In the foyer, peering this way and that through the crush, he had been absurdly worried. He was still concerned about her, though more critical of himself now. It just would not do. He was making a fool of himself. In no time at all now he would become ridiculous.

A wave of music reached him. An eclipse of some sort threw a shadow over Anna's face. The amber dusk had changed to a steel-blue night, and when Burton glanced at the stage, he saw that the scene had moved to the gloomy lake of the swans.

He made an effort to give attention to the ballet. The moment for Babette's entrance was near. Anna leaned forward, expectantly. Burton found himself in a curious state of anxiety. It was nothing to him whether the new ballerina triumphed or failed, except that Anna wished for the triumph. He turned to look at her. When he saw the stage again, the white Princess of the swans was emerging from the painted forest, fluttering towards the Prince, checking.

There was no sign from the audience to indicate that a great moment had arrived and passed, for tradition demanded an unbroken silence till the curtain fell. Babette seemed a tiny figure on that enormous stage, solitary, isolated in the white glare of the converging spots that followed her movements.

Burton had seen her in two or three secondary roles in other ballets and had liked her dancing. Perhaps he would not have noticed her if Anna had not pointed her out. He enjoyed ballet occasionally, but knew little about it. He tried now to compare Babette to Vera Kurtz, but all he derived from this exercise was the conviction that Babette was very different. She was airy and graceful, she moved with precision, she had a dark, youthful loveliness, but somehow there was an effect of effort in her work. The Swan Princess was beautiful, but without soul. She came down stage on twinkling points. Then something went wrong.

There was an audible gasp from some of the audience. Burton felt Anna's fingers close tightly on his forearm and heard the whisper of a shocked exclamation. For a fraction of time a terrified Odette stood flat-soled in her ballet shoes. Then the Prince masked her fault, moved towards her with a commanding gesture, and she was on her toes again. She went on without further fault, but Burton could see that her work was dead. She was straining to remember each sequence of steps, and when the curtain fell, the little applause, polite or sympathetic, was cut off by a buzz of talk.

Anna was white-faced, suffering for her friend. "I must talk to her," she said. "If she doesn't pull herself together, she'll never get through the next act." They joined the throng that moved towards the foyer.

"She'll be all right when she's over her nerves." Burton wanted to be reassuring. "She's very young and it's a big job. Even old hands go down with stage fright."

"Babette does not get stage fright. She knows the work backwards and she is a good dancer. She can dance Kurtz off her toes. Tonight she is as clumsy as an elephant. Her mind is . . ."

They were separated at the doorway; came together in the foyer.

"What's the matter with her mind?" he asked.

"Nothing. She is worrying. I must talk to her."

"Shall I go with you?"

"They will not let you in. They are very strict. For me it is different. I am known. Please wait here for me. I'll not be long."

She moved away quickly and people came between them. When he reached the grand staircase she was halfway down. She paused in the crush to draw on the coat she had brought from the auditorium. Two young men pushed towards her and spoke to her. For a moment the trio formed a stationary knot in the stream of people. The young men were solemn-faced, and Burton thought that they too must be concerned about the fiasco of Babette Trepleva's debut. Perhaps they were all of one set; certainly they seemed quite familiar with one another. They argued gravely. Then one of the men grasped Anna by the elbow and went down the stairs with her. The other man watched them, then followed slowly.

Burton hesitated. There was a crowd in the bar and the place was overheated. He, too, went down the staircase and out on to the great portico. He looked for Anna and her escort without expecting to see them. The other young man was standing at the end of the colonnade as if waiting for their return.

It was a clear night, but with a nip of winter in the air, and only a few of the audience had come from the warm interior. Burton lit a cigarette. He looked out across Opera Place and thought how similar it was to the wide square in front of the Bolshoi in Moscow. He walked to one end of the colonnade, turned, and encountered Mervan of the Paris Press Agency.

"Well, my dear colleague, I didn't know you were an *aficionado.*" Mervan was patronising as ever; the sneer in his voice quite an accomplishment. "What do you think of the new ballerina? Not quite an Ulanova, is she? I'm afraid we'll have to endure the veteran Kurtz to the arthritic end."

"Give the kid a chance," Burton said. "The show's not over."

"She's finished, my dear fellow, finished. A face alone is not enough. Apropos of faces, who is the little lady of the evening? She's enchanting. You must introduce me. Not an American visitor? I hear there's one due, on a bicycle. I'm instructed by Paris to interview her. Don't tell me that lovely girl has been cycling across Europe!"

"She's my secretary," Burton said coldly.

"You mean she's a local product?" Mervan stared. "That makes a difference. If I were you, my dear, I'd be rather cautious about these local girls. I suppose Glover warned you before he left. I mention it because you're comparatively new here."

"I've been alive a few years."

"Don't misunderstand me. The police system is quite thorough. Personally, in a country like this, I prefer to work alone. That way they can't get anything on you."

"What makes you think they could get anything on me?"

"You must not be so sensitive. I'm merely telling you that I like to keep on the safe side."

"Very wise." Burton threw the end of his cigarette into a receptacle. "I'll have to be getting back to my seat."

The crowd was thinning in the foyer. He looked inside the auditorium. Anna had not returned. He waited at the head of the staircase till the last bell went. Back in his seat he watched the doorway till the lights went down, but he no longer expected the girl. He remembered that there was quite a lot of business in the ballroom scene before Babette would come on as Odile, the temptress, and it seemed most likely that Anna had decided to stay with her until she was called to the stage.

He was bored by the long series of *divertissements* that opened the act. Only when Babette came on was he interested again, and then the change in her astonished him. The transformation by costume and make-up into the daughter of the bad magician was the least part of that change. She had become an artist, sure of her technique, confident in the effect of every gesture and step. Perhaps she would never be placed among the great ones, but with this dramatic recovery she had certainly arrived. The audience appreciated the feat. The curtain brought unstinted applause.

Burton looked vainly round the house for Anna, feeling a touch of annoyance. If she wanted to spend the rest of the evening back stage with Babette, she might at least let him know. He had an impulse to walk out now, but curbed it and stayed for the last act. His annoyance increased. He was angry with the girl; angry with himself for putting up with her treatment of him, but presently this mood gave way to anxiety. It was not in her character to behave so abominably. Something had happened to prevent her rejoining him and she had found it impossible or unwise to send him a message.

Sesnik?

Suddenly the gift of the tickets, after his failure to procure seats in the normal way, took on a new light. The police worked in peculiar ways. Because of Trovic, Sesnik was suspicious of everyone connected with the *Star-Dispatch*. The man had asked about Sokolny. Perhaps he had caused Anna to be taken to his office for questioning. That encounter with the two on the staircase . . .

The stage was blanked out for him; he was deaf to the music. He rose in the darkened place and started towards the doorway. When he reached the foyer, he realised that the performance had just ended, and the noise that came from the auditorium told him that the crowd were cheering the new ballerina. He still looked for Anna, hoping that she was waiting for him, but the foyer was deserted. He went to the cloakroom for his coat and hat. He watched the lobby through which she might pass; there was no sign of her. Out under the portico he hesitated a moment, then strode along the side street to the back of the theatre. When he turned the corner he saw her. She was standing near the stage door and the man who had gone with her from the foyer was holding her by one arm, possessively, with the possessiveness of a guardian.

A car came slowly along the narrow street, passed Burton, and moved in the direction of the stage door. It was an old car, battered and scarred. As it pulled up at the kerb, the possessive man, the guardian, drew Anna away from the doorway.

Burton called her name, and she saw him. She halted, then took a step towards him. The guardian restrained her and she turned on him. Angrily, Burton thought. What was certain was that she tugged to free her arm. Burton ran, but he was still some distance off. He saw the car door open. An arm reached out to grasp the girl as the guardian hustled her across the pavement. She was drawn and pushed into the vehicle, the guardian followed her, the door was slammed, and the car moved off along the street.

It was final. She was beyond reach, but Burton kept running after the car. Perhaps he had the hope that he would find an autocab at the end of the back street; that he might follow the car, overtake it. He saw the red taillight disappear round the corner. When he reached the corner, there was no autocab and the car was out of sight.

He halted as if he had come up against a solid obstacle. He was aware of people in front of him and behind him, coming from the Opera House, moving across the road. His first dismay was paralysing. He tried to think what he should do, but there seemed to be nothing he could do. He could not go to the police and complain that the girl had been forcibly taken away in a car. She might be under arrest. If not, an appeal to the police might be disastrous to her, for there was the alternative supposition that she was involved with Trovic or men like Trovic. She had shown no fear of the two who had accosted her in the Opera House. It was by no means certain that she had gone unwillingly to the car. Burton could be sure only that she had been prevented from speaking to him, but he felt in his bones that she was in danger, and the thought of it made him cold.

Turning, he went slowly back to the stage door, pushing through a press of people on the pavement. He spoke to the elderly doorkeeper. He said he wished to see Babette Trepleva.

"But that is impossible." The doorkeeper shook his head emphatically.

"I am a representative of the foreign press. I wish to interview the new ballerina." Burton knew so little of the language he had to labour over the phrases.

Again the doorkeeper shook his head. There was strictly no admittance. Interviews with artists were permitted only by arrangement with the Ministry of Propaganda.

"I am also a friend. Will you please take my card to the lady?"

The doorkeeper frowned at the five-dollar bill held out to him and this time shook his grey head with conscious pride. This was no longer the old regime.

Burton crumpled the bill in his hand, shoved it into a pocket, and drew back into the crowd, hoping that he would be able to intercept the dancer. Others left the theatre, but not Babette. Then it was stated that she had departed by another door, and her disappointed admirers began to disperse. Once more Burton felt the dismay of frustration. Babette might have some explanation of the episode of the car, but he did not know where to find Babette. If he asked for her address, the doorkeeper, or any other official of the opera, would no doubt refer him to the Propaganda Ministry.

He turned from the stage door, his anxiety mounting. He went through the streets knowing that the safety of Anna Maras was the only thing that mattered to him. The whisky at the Metropole tasted like turpentine, but he had a drink, and then another.

Swinging from fear for the girl to a mood of optimism, he came round to the view that he had exaggerated the whole business. Anna had driven off with friends, possibly to visit someone or to take supper. She had wanted to explain this to him, but her friends had been in too much of a hurry. By now, no doubt, she was safe at home, and tomorrow she would try to apologise for her behaviour. But he wasn't going to wait till tomorrow.

Anna had a room on the western edge of the city. He found an autocab and gave the driver the address. The janitress knew him, and grumbled only slightly at being dragged from her quarters. She believed that Anna had not come in, but, on his insistence, went upstairs to make sure. She was right. She shrugged it away. It was nothing to bother about. The whole house was inhabited by night owls. Night owls!

Burton walked the pavement outside, waiting for her. His optimism lasted for another hour. Then he knew it was false, and fear claimed him again. The conviction that she was in danger was stronger, and there was nothing he could do about it.

He went back to the Metropole and drank more whisky.

# VI

Shifting from one foot to the other, Sokolny was like a rocking horse with the rockers set sideways instead of head to tail. The prominent Adam's apple moved with each shift as if he were swallowing. The big dark eyes in the pale wedge face reminded Burton of a frightened rabbit, and he was in no mood for rabbits. The pick-me-up he had taken had failed him. His head hammered and his stomach felt hollow.

Sokolny said, "He asked me questions about Trovic. Over and over, till I am dazed in my mind with the light shining in my eyes. So I tell him. I tell him over and over that I know nothing about Trovic; that he is a man who works for you. Then he asked me—"

"Forget about Sesnik." Burton cut in on the maundering statement. "Tell me just what the girl said. Give me her own words if you can remember them."

It was difficult for Sokolny to make the mental switch. He meditated. "She says, 'Sokolny, is Mr. Burton there?' and I answer her that you are late this morning and what is the matter with her that she too is not at work, and if she wants you she'd better try the hotel. Then she says, 'I don't want him. I wish you to give him message. My father is sick and I go to him. I don't know when I will be in the office.' "

"What did she mean by that? Today? Tomorrow? Next week?"

Sokolny shrugged and made a gesture of helplessness. "Before I can ask, she hangs up the receiver. Perhaps she will be in this afternoon."

"Where is her father? I didn't know he was still alive. Who is he?"

"Anton Maras. He was professor of modern history at the university. Now he retires and lives in the country."

"Where in the country?"

Sokolny shook his head. "Perhaps I find out from the university?"

"Yes. Find out at once. Don't telephone. Go."

Was it really conceivable that Sesnik would be tapping the line?

Burton wandered to the window and looked down the river at the Gothic spires of the police building.

Anything was conceivable. It was conceivable that no one could depend on his neighbour; that under the calm surface of life there was a spreading sore of mistrust. Anna Maras doubted Sokolny, so she telephoned to give him this false story of a father's illness. But perhaps it was for his benefit as well as Sokolny's. She did not trust him either, and she could have no realisation of the anxiety that had led him into the crazy courses of the night.

At least he now had what assurance he could derive from the fact that she had telephoned to the office. She was a free agent, since she could use the telephone for her own purposes. . . .

But the argument ended unresolved. An alternative thought brought back all the fears. Anything was conceivable, and it might be that she had been forced to speak her message to Sokolny.

Burton went to the filter and took a long drink of cold water.

Sokolny returned at one o'clock. Professor Maras lived outside the village of Tolnitz, which was a few kilometres beyond the outer suburbs to the north. The last news the university had of him was that he was in good health.

Little was added to Burton's knowledge, nothing taken from his suspicion, but now, as his head cleared, he became more and more anxious. He left Sokolny in charge of the office and went once more by autocab to the house where Anna had her room.

"She has not been in," the janitress informed him. "Perhaps she has gone to Tolnitz. She goes sometimes."

On the way back to the office Burton noticed a small black car behind his cab. He gave a new direction to his driver, and a little later changed it again. The small black car was still following when the cab pulled up at the office building.

He did not enter. Instead he walked to the Metropole and ordered black coffee and a sandwich. He ate only half the sandwich. Leaving the place, he ran into Mervan.

"So our little ballerina made a big hit after all," the Frenchman commented. "I wish I had stayed, but really I was too discouraged. Now the papers are enthusiastic about her. Tershin calls her a new Lepeshinskaya. It is a black eye for the Kurtz, eh?" He put out a restraining hand. "Why are you in so much of a hurry? Come in and drink with me."

"Too busy," Burton grunted. "Sorry."

He was indeed in a hurry, striding with a purpose. He had an impulse to go to Tolnitz, but was afraid of the black car that had followed him. He would make no move until he had found out if Babette knew anything, and he would go to Babette quite openly. He crossed the Alexis Bridge to the Propaganda Ministry and sought a friendly official in the Foreign Press Department.

"I wish to have a talk with Babette Trepleva," he announced.

The official looked puzzled. "I beg your pardon, Mr. Burton. Who is Babette Trepleva?"

"You should read your newspapers, Gregor. She made a sensation at the ballet last night. The critic Tershin says she is a new Lepeshinskaya." "I do not follow these things very closely. Why do you wish to see this dancer?"

"To get her life story and some pictures."

Gregor frowned doubtfully. "These people are difficult. They do not like to have one artist singled out unless the State accords some distinction. It causes jealousy, and jealousy is disrupting. The ballet in particular . . ." Gregor gesticulated, seeking the elusive English term. "The ballet is cagey."

"You can talk them over."

"I fear that is impossible."

"You don't realize the importance, Gregor," Burton argued. "The ballet is one of your finest cultural assets. Properly exploited, it will bring you valuable publicity."

"I can arrange for you to see the leading woman. What is her name?—Kurtz?"

"Kurtz is out. Trepleva is romance, the young dancer's leap to stardom. That's story. That's what I want for the magazine section. I'll put it on the plane tonight; next Sunday all America will be reading about your ballet. The stress will be on the whole organisation. We'll have a big layout. Kurtz included."

Gregor was moved. "I'll have to consult. I'll let you know in the morning."

"Consult right away. The morning will be too late."

The consultation took some time, but a little after four Burton was at the Opera House asking for a man named Varaban. A group of dancers were at work in an enormous room, some practising a series of steps in the middle of the floor, others exercising at the *barres* that ran round the walls. First Varaban was detached from confusion, then Babette was led forward, a shabby figure in an old blouse and patched tights.

Varaban's introduction was positively courtly, of the old regime. A supplicant was presented to a queen, and the supplicant prayed that the queen would give no indication that she had met him briefly in a teashop with Anna Maras. He moved a finger towards his lips and she checked, looked puzzled for an instant, and murmured a few formal words in her own tongue. Varaban could have seen nothing. He led the way to a small office, and the interview proceeded under his guidance. He was interpreter and watchdog in one. He considered the questions before he put them to the dancer. He censored her replies if they did not suit him. But this newspaper man was easily satisfied and very soon signified that he had enough copy for his purpose.

"I want some pictures," he said. "The best shots you have of Miss Trepleva."

"Pictures!" Varaban was scandalised. "Pictures are not permitted."

"I believe I have the consent of the Ministry."

Varaban spoke to Babette. She answered sharply, commandingly.

"I will consult," he told Burton. "Come with me."

They went back to the rehearsal room, and then Burton found the chance for which he had come. Varaban left them.

Babette spoke no English, but her French was fairly fluent.

"What has happened to Anna?" he asked her.

"Why do you come to me like this?" she complained.

"You saw Anna last night?"

"Yes."

"What did she say to you? Why didn't she come back to her seat?"

The dancers in the centre of the room were still working on their sequences of steps. A pianist banged out a tune with strongly marked rhythm. Commands in a harsh voice punctuated the music. Along the *barres* the students were busy.

Babette looked round anxiously.

"We must not talk here," she said. "It is dangerous." "I must know about Anna. If she is not back at the office tomorrow, I shall go to the police."

"No! For the love of God, no!"

The fear in her voice told him something, but there was nothing reassuring in the knowledge. The girl was making an effort to hide her agitation. Varaban was coming back, striding lithely down the long room to the rhythm of the piano. His quick eyes were fixed on Babette and Burton.

"I must know," Burton insisted.

"He will see," she whispered. "Tonight I will be at home. Thirty-nine Katerina Street. The name is my name. Make sure you are not followed."

Varaban said, "We are taking up the picture question with the Ministry. You will want a Swan *Lake* pose, no doubt?"

"Yes," Burton agreed. "The Swan Princess."

# VII

He did not bother himself about the man who was on his trail when he left the Opera House. His movements were normal and could be checked by all the police in the country for all he cared. The trouble would begin when he started on his visit to Babette, for then it would be necessary to shake off the shadow. Otherwise Sesnik would have some new questions for him, and Babette, too, might be in an awkward position. The best plan, as he saw it, would be to behave absolutely normally until he started for Katerina Street.

Nothing had happened at the office except that Sokolny had had another attack of toothache. Burton sent him home, looked over a few news items that had come in, then started to punch out the ballerina story on his typewriter. It was unimportant. It was merely something to satisfy the Foreign Press Department when they checked up with the censorship. He left the office at seven, called at the Metropole for a drink, then walked to his hotel. Normally he would have gone up to his room and come down again when dinner was served. He followed the usual course as far as his floor, then, unobserved, went along the corridor, down the service stairs, and out by a rear doorway. Two tests satisfied him that he was not being followed, and he then joined the queue at a bus stop.

The house in Katerina Street was an apartment building in the old style, slightly pretentious in a middle-class way and more than a little dilapidated. After the clear crisp air of the November night, it had a stuffy smell of steam heat and oil on parquet floors, but Burton was used to it by the time he had climbed four flights to the Treplev flat.

A small grey-haired man, worried-looking, unfriendly, opened the door. Possibly a government clerk in one of the higher categories.

He said resentfully, "My daughter expects you. You may come in." It might have been, "You are here to bring trouble upon us, but I cannot prevent you."

The place was clean and looked comfortable. The living room was obviously much used, and there were signs of recent occupation: wrinkled chair covers, rumpled cushions, cigarette ends in ash trays, a newspaper cast down on the carpet.

Treplev picked up the newspaper and took it with him.

"Please wait," he said. "My daughter will not be long."

Burton looked round. There were framed enlargements of family portraits on the walls; pictures of Babette at all ages from cradle to tutu. You could follow her growth from the spindle-legged child in tarlatan to the lovely creature in the skirts of *Les Sylphides*.

Babette came. She was in a grave mood that lent an almost tragic overtone to her dark loveliness. She was the condemned Antigone, the lost Giselle, so different from the gay Babette he had met with Anna in the teashop. She said, "Monsieur Burton, I gave you this address because I have a very urgent request to make. I want you to leave me alone, and I know that Anna wishes the same for herself."

"Does she say so? Is that a message from her?"

"She would say it if she were here. As it is, I have to say it to you. We have our own lives to live in this country. How we live them is our affair. You have to get news for your paper, but you will not wish to make things difficult for us. You have been kind to Anna and I know you are friendly to me. I know you would help us if you could, but your visit to the school this afternoon might have made great trouble for me."

"How could that be, mademoiselle? It had official sanction."

"Monsieur Burton, you are under suspicion. I have heard about your call to the Police Judiciary. I know you personally have done nothing to help refugees to get across the frontier, but that is not the point. Other innocent people may be involved if you try to interfere in things you do not understand. You may be watched, I don't know. It was foolish of me to give you this address. If there is any question about your visit, I will say that you came to get more details for your interview."

"I'm being watched all right," Burton admitted, "but I know positively that I was not followed tonight."

She nodded slowly. "I suppose I am too nervous, but we are all so nervous. Sesnik knows that I am a friend of Anna, but that is all. He has left me alone."

"Does that mean that Anna is under suspicion?"

"We do not know. She has done nothing to warrant suspicion except to work in your office."

"In the name of heaven, what is this? Does Sesnik think I'm running an escape agency? Where is Anna? What has happened to her?"

"I don't know."

"You must have some idea. What did she have to tell you last night?" "She came to tell me that everything was all right. I had been so worried, I could not dance. We talked, and I felt better.

"Why were you so worried if you had nothing on your conscience?"

"I have tried to explain it to you, monsieur." There was an agony of anxiety in her frown. "You must understand."

"I understand that there is a lot you haven't told me, Babette," he answered gently. "If you and Anna are in danger, I want to help you." He hesitated. "I have become very fond of Anna. I must find her. Where did she go when she left you last night?"

"She said nothing. I thought she was going back to you. You must wait. Perhaps she is at Tolnitz with her father. You will hear from her when it is possible."

It was no use. He could get nothing more out of her and it was obvious that she wanted him to go. When he rose, she moved towards the door of the room. She had left it ajar. Now she opened it widely, then stood still with her hand on the knob. Burton heard a key inserted in the lock of the flat door across the narrow hall. The door was thrust open and a man entered quickly. He was muffled up in a coat with a high collar and a felt hat was pulled low over his brow, but Burton saw something of his face.

"You!" Babette cried out in alarm. "Why have you come here?"

Burton blinked and looked again.

The man was Trovic.

# VIII

The light from the hanging lamp in the hall showed a colourless Babette in a sudden agony of mind. Burton interpreted the look in her dark eyes as dismay. There was bewilderment too, and for a moment she was utterly confused. She stared at the man, who had let himself in, then turned to Burton, making a fluttering gesture towards the door with her hands. She wanted him to go at once, but Trovic was barring the way, and it seemed that he too was highly disconcerted. If so, he recovered quickly. He took off his hat and threw back the collar of his coat. He greeted Babette familiarly, then faced Burton.

"Good evening." He spoke in English. "I had not hoped to meet you so soon. I trust the article from Kazyos was satisfactory?"

"Thoroughly. I'm not using it." Burton watched him closely, ready for any move that might come.

"Not using it? Why?"

"Mr. Sesnik might find it too entertaining."

"You are solicitous for Sesnik?"

"I'm full of solicitude."

Burton was aware of Babette's anxiety as she looked from one to the other of them, trying to understand the English.

Trovic turned to her. "Leave us, Babette. We have business to discuss."

"You were mad to come back. The police will take you." She spoke quickly, but Burton made out the gist of it.

"Leave us!" Trovic insisted, and she backed along the passage, watching him.

He came into the living-room and closed the door. He threw his hat on a chair, but kept his coat buttoned up. His right hand reached down into the pocket and stayed there.

"What are you doing in this house?" he demanded.

Burton told him. "Perhaps you can tell me where I can find Anna Maras," he suggested.

"I know nothing of Anna Maras."

"I'd like to believe that, for her sake, but I'm not that simple." He looked searchingly at the man's stern face. "You don't have to keep on fondling that gun in your pocket," he added. "You can't use it here. It would be too awkward for you, wouldn't it?"

Trovic withdrew an open hand and slapped the pocket to show that it was empty. "Your imagination is too active, my friend," he said. "All the same, it is best that you keep yourself out of danger."

He had shaved off his small moustache. His hair had been dyed to a flaxen hue, cut fairly close, parted, and brushed down in a bang over his forehead. He had done something to his eyebrows, too, but he could not disguise the eyes. They had given him away to Burton and they would betray him to anyone who had observed their peculiarity. Not that there was anything unusual about the grey-green colour of them. It was the expression behind them.

"It is you who should keep yourself out of danger," Burton retorted. "Seznik is very concerned about you."

"Sesnik thinks I am out of the country."

"When did you learn that?"

"Learn it? I played him a trick. I planned it."

"I don't think so, pal." Burton shook his head. "You didn't know what Sesnik thought when you sent me your article on the Horse Fair. You wouldn't be that crazy, would you? The Kazyos stunt was just another of your tricks to get somebody else across the frontier. The refugee happened to be of your build and the police jumped at the wrong conclusion."

"So you think you are intelligent, Mr. Burton? Will you be intelligent enough not to betray me?"

"I don't see why I should betray you. I don't like the way you used me. I don't like the tricks you played on Glover, either, but I'm not taking sides."

"There were no tricks on Glover," Trovic asserted sharply. "He was in it from the first. He wanted to get a man away, one of his friends. It was I who arranged it."

"That was the first assignment?" "If it was, what of it?"

"I'm beginning to understand." Burton stared, challenging Trovic to meet his gaze. "In the other cases, you just blackmailed him into helping."

"You may ask Glover about that when you see him." Trovic looked away. "It is nothing to me what words you use Your newspaper cannot escape its share, and if Sesnik ever finds out what I know, there will be a lot of trouble." He faced Burton again, and this time his was the challenging gaze. "You say you are not taking sides, Mr. Burton. It is not true. You are taking sides with me. If not, it will be necessary to make sure that you keep silent."

The peculiarity about his eyes was the fever behind them. It was always there, smouldering; it blazed up as if a fire had been fanned and you looked into the eyes of a fanatic. If there had ever been any humanity in him, it had long ago been destroyed.

Involuntarily Burton shivered. He was not afraid for himself. He was afraid for Trovic and the people who were close to him. He knew fanaticism and what it could do. Trovic's kind would never enmesh themselves in thoughts of right and wrong, of praise and blame.

"I'm not taking sides with anyone."

"What have you done with the story from Kazyos?" Trovic demanded.

"Burned it."

"So! That is enough for me. You have committed yourself, my friend. You stand for the same things that Glover stood for, but I think you are not so foolish. That is the only difference. I appreciate what you have done. It will be made up to you. You shall have a story, but not about a horse fair in a mountain village. It will be something big, something that will shake the foundations of the country and spread fear across its borders." "Get across the border yourself before Sesnik catches up with you," Burton advised him. "Your game's at an end."

"My game is just beginning." Trovic almost declaimed the line. "I am safe because I do not exist. I have escaped, through the mines and the wire. To Sesnik I am dead, and you do not shoot dead men."

"Be careful someone doesn't bring you back to life."

"Have no fear. I will see to it. So long as you forget that you have seen me, you will be as safe as I am. Go back to your office and wait for the story. Then you will bring me to life and send my name round the world."

Burton could imagine the desperate dream. The body was puny, ill-nourished; it might have a certain wiry strength supported by the fanatical will to endure, but this man could do nothing against the system. Sesnik would have him before the flaxen hair needed another wash of dye. Yet, he believed in himself and must follow his faith to the end. The fires burned out the lines of weariness and anxiety in his face, and he was again the young man of the Turgenev comedy, the young man grown ardent in devotion to a cause. He followed what? The promise of a headline?

Burton shrugged. "Don't tell me any more," he said. "You'll spoil it for me. Let the story break. Let me get the full effect, like the other suckers."

"You Americans have no courage, so you must always scoff." The fire began to die down. "It is no matter. I can trust you." He moved towards the door and Burton followed him. In the hall, he said, "You will have no further business with Babette Trepleva. If you are involved with Sesnik, you must not involve others."

"Listen, son," Burton said gently, "don't give me orders. I don't want to involve anybody in anything, but I'm going to find Anna Maras. Is that clear?"

"Clear? But of course. Anna Maras is your secretary. That is all. And naturally, you are careful to have no other thought of her. So you need not worry. No doubt she will return to her employment when she is ready. I think it is that her father is ill. He is not a strong man. He has been persecuted all his life by Sesnik. The daughter is very anxious about him, but she has her own salvation to work out. She does not need your help. None of us need your help. We know what to do. Everything is clear. Quite clear."

He closed the flat door gently, so that it made no sound. Burton walked slowly down the stairs.

# IX

When the shadowers picked him up again, they would hang on like leeches. He looked up and down the street curiously. No spy was in sight, but battalions might be hidden in doorways. When he moved, he could not rid himself of a feeling of apprehension. He turned the first corner and waited. No one came after him. The result was negative again at the next corner. Down by the canal an autocab discharged a fare. Burton shouted to the driver and waited.

"Take me to Tolnitz," he instructed the man. "The home of Professor Maras, outside Tolnitz."

"Where outside Tolnitz?" the driver demanded.

Burton shrugged. "When you get there, ask."

The journey to Tolnitz took half an hour. In a few more minutes the driver stopped at a gateway to a property that looked like a walled-off remnant of woodland in a wide stretch of arable.

"Wait," Burton instructed the man.

The details revealed by the moonlight were not inviting. The wall was high and wide and beyond it stood tall pines and wide-branched cedars. The gate of wooden pickets was falling to pieces. The hinges were rusted through and sagging. Burton eased the gate back, squeezed through the opening, and found the remains of a tiled path.

He followed it cautiously, stepping through dried grasses beneath the tall, dark trees. It seemed a long way, but it could not have been more than a few yards before he came to the end of the trees and saw the house across the wide space of what had once been a terraced garden. It was a plain flat walled house of two storeys, white in the moonlight. It was a large house with many windows and all the windows were guarded by fastened jalousies. It looked empty, and he wondered if the driver had been misdirected.

He hesitated, then moved forward. The terraces had been laid out in different patterns of brickwork. There were small beds at intervals and ornamental urns and vases, and it had once been a place of formal neatness; now it was a rank wilderness of weeds and overgrown vines. The weeds thrust up between the bricks, and the grasses trailed in disorder from the vases.

He approached and went close enough to see the weather bleached wood where the paint had peeled from the jalousies. Light showed dimly through the slats of one pair.

He rang the doorbell. He was about to ring a second time when a lamp was switched on in the hall. The door opened a fraction, held on a chain, and Burton answered a thin-voiced inquiry by giving his name. He was admitted by a white-haired man in a dressing gown that must have given him many years of service.

"I am Anton Maras," the old man said in English. "I have heard of you from my daughter. I am honoured by your visit, even if I have to say that it is unexpected. This way, please. My study is the only warm place. We are short of fuel. We have so many shortages, but that of fuel is the worst. Will you drink? Slivovitz is good when you are cold inside." The long room was lined with tall, heavy bookcases. The floor was dark with a faded red carpet. A great desk, burdened with books and papers, stood close to the tiled stove, and the only light came from a green-shaded standard lamp on one side of the desk. A small blue flame burned under a silver tea urn on the table where Maras kept his liquor and an assortment of glasses. Coming from the icy air of the hallway, the study was warm, but not warm enough. There was a mustiness of books in the air and the smell of cooked paprika. A saucepan stood on the top ledge of the stove.

Burton said, "I understood you were ill, sir. I came to inquire about you and to ask when Anna would return to the office."

"Anna?" Maras repeated the name with a questioning inflection, then found the right answer. "It is these sudden attacks. The only thing about them is that they pass quickly. Otherwise I endure; but you must understand, Mr. Burton, that in common with the rest of humanity I am under sentence of death. My time approaches. . . . Your health, Mr. Burton."

"Then it's true that Anna came to you last night?"

"Why should it not be true?"

There was evasion in the manner as well as in the words. Burton felt an irritation that ran towards anger. He could not get anywhere with these people—Anna herself, or her father. They were full of retreats and evasions. They always had something to hide; something that it might be very dangerous to uncover. Better say nothing more. Better get out while there was still time. Anna Maras was nothing to him. Or should be nothing. He had a job. He was a newspaper man.

Maras drank. "Anna is a faithful daughter." He stared at his glass. "It is unfortunate that the old must put such a burden on youth. In the days of stability—we called it stability—we could be pushed into a safe corner, but today we hang like chains on the necks of the young. I wish to set Anna free, yet I pray for strength to finish my work first. I am very near the end. Very near."

Burton fidgeted. Old men were like drunks. You never knew exactly how to deal with them.

"Perhaps you'll permit me to speak to Anna."

"She is not here." Maras said it quite casually, with even a suggestion of indifference. "Please sit down, Mr. Burton. I have been wanting to talk to you for some time. Draw up to the stove."

He stood against the light of the standard lamp for a moment, a thin, bowed figure with the white hair fluffed out from his head like a halo. The old brown gown hung upon him loosely. He shuffled forward in his slippers and sat down on the lower ledge of the stove.

"It is about Anna," he said. "If anything happens to me, she will be alone. Perhaps she is already alone, and a little lost. She has told you, no doubt, that she had been in your country?"

"No. I had no idea."

"You are surprised that she has not spoken? It is not surprising to me. We suppress the old loyalties and loves in an effort to identify ourselves more wholly with the new. The process is not always effective. I do not know how it is with Anna, except that she is sometimes secretive, and this suggests doubts. A going back in thought, shall we say?"

He frowned. The old face was full of trouble. "Who should not doubt, when logic itself is like a spy at the door, waiting to betray us. I sometimes feel I will live to hear peace cry havoc, and I have not long to live, though I have lived too long. I have seen too many changes, inside myself as well as outside. Years ago, Mr. Burton, I had a very dear friend. He is dead to me now, and I sometimes think he is dead to himself. He has become an apparatus, a symbol; all that was human in him has passed into legend. He is a recluse like myself, but next week he will emerge. He will drive into the city and the people will cheer his name. He will take the salute as the troops march past. He will be in the State Box on the gala night at the opera. You will send cables to your paper, describing his progress. You have not yet seen him in person, have you?"

"You mean the President?"

"Yes. We were at the university together. Let me get you a glass of tea."

"Thank you, no. You were speaking of your daughter."

"Of course. I have a daughter. How stupid of me to forget. Her mother died in your country. I was lecturing; teaching history while history itself rushed by. Anna was happy in America. I think she loved it there. We should have stayed, but my son was here, and I was anxious about him. My sister wished Anna to remain with her in Boston, but the child was unwilling to part from me; also, she was eager to see her brother again. Peter was three years her senior and she had always idolised him."

Maras paused a moment, closing his eyes.

Burton said, "I didn't know she had a brother. She has never mentioned him."

The old man ignored the interruption. "So we came home," he went on. "We arrived just in time for the outbreak of war. Anna was thirteen then. Later we had the Nazi invasion, and before the end she was old enough to follow her brother and join the Resistance. Even the children learned to kill Nazis. I don't mean that Anna carried a gun. That was Peter's part. He was a leader. They caught him and tortured him and left his body in the gutter."

Burton waited through another pause. All he could think of to say seemed stupid. He said nothing.

"Anna became hard and bitter. She had done office work, collecting, editing, writing. Now she was there when anyone was needed for a dangerous task. The war had become a personal war, and when the enemy fled in defeat, I had a terrible anxiety for her. She had specialised in planned hatred, and that takes a long while to get over. But Anna was all right. She had passed through her grief and could look forward to realising a new life. She took the transition easier than some of her comrades. It was not so easy to take the political schisms that followed. The fanatics raised a clamour, demanding loyalty to this and that, and their fanaticism has not diminished. It is the inevitable harvest, Mr. Burton. I don't know where Anna stands today. I don't know how she evades or satisfies the conflicting demands. I know that she is sane and good, and I wish she were out of it, back in America. She has given up enough of her youth. It is time she married and settled down to the proper business of a young woman."

"She seems to like her work," Burton remarked uneasily.

"I worry about her." Maras frowned again. "It is because you have been a good friend that I appeal to you, Mr. Burton. Try to get her out of it. I will persuade her to leave me, if you will help. You see my precarious state. Tomorrow a sudden attack may end it. Or there may be an accident. I grow very forgetful. I have this drug, you see." He produced a small bottle of tablets from a pocket of his gown. "Sometimes I have great difficulty in remembering whether I have taken it. You see . . . ?" He left the sentence hanging in the air.

"Hadn't you better count the tablets so that you'll be sure?" Burton said sharply. "You may be more important to Anna than anybody else."

"You think so?" The old man's voice had a chill note. He was disappointed. "I can understand that you have no wish to mix yourself up in our affairs. There would be too much risk for you in your position. Perhaps if I appeal to the President I can myself arrange matters." "If you know him so well."

"Yes. I thank you for your visit, Mr. Burton. You must forgive me for keeping you so long."

In the icebox of a hall Burton said, "By the way, Professor, do you know a man called Pero Trovic?"

"No." Maras shook his head quickly.

"Or an Andreas Nimsky?"

"I have never heard of either of them. I am sorry."

Anton Maras was an honest man. It was very easy to tell when he was lying.

"Good night, Mr. Burton," he said. "I am grateful for your visit, for your concern. I am sure Anna will return to work in the morning."

# X

She did not return. Sokolny came in with a swollen jaw. Self-pity oozed from him as he rocked from foot to foot, but Burton was getting tired of Sokolny. Anna was right. The man was untrustworthy, a weakling. He would break down if serious trouble threatened him. Better sack him before he came walking in with disaster in his pocket. Turn him out into the snow to look for that lost kopeck.

It was falling and lifting and waltzing outside the window, the first snow. You looked at the domes of St. Trophimus through a white-dotted veil, and the more distant of the ten bridges were scarcely visible. But it was as yet no more than a light flurry. The pavements were clear. The Dreva flowed sullenly.

If Sokolny were fired, what would happen to the man? He was so incompetent, so vulnerable, poor devil! You might make up your mind a dozen times to pay him off, and always you'd be up against that half-fawning trust in you. "Where did you pick up that story about the new escape plan?" Burton demanded.

Sokolny teetered. "You will excuse me, sir. It was established by Mr. Glover that my sources are to be confidential. I have friends who tell me things. It is on the understanding that no names are to be mentioned."

"How is the escape going to be managed?"

"Of that I am not yet informed. It will be something unusual. It will make a sensational story."

"For the censor to tear up. When is the business to be staged?"

Sokolny hesitated. "Near the end of the anniversary celebrations. Some time, I think, after the parade of the Army next week. Many people will be travelling. The delegates and the deputations will be going home."

"That won't make it any easier for unauthorised travel."

"The permits will be arranged."

"But none of them through this office."

"I have already told you, sir, I had nothing to do with Trovic's deception." He went on protesting at length.

There had been a time when Burton would have accepted the vehement denials, the earnest protestations, the injured innocence, but now he was developing the professional scepticism of an examining magistrate.

"How long were you employed by Glover?" he said eventually.

"All the time he was here. I was with Mr. Pendleton, before Mr. Glover came."

"Pendleton opened the office after the war?"

"Yes, sir, but I was not with him from the beginning. He had a man named Weiss, a deserter from the Nazis, who turned out to be a police spy."

"What sort of spy are you?"

"Sir, you know I have nothing to do with the police. Do you think I would be able to get information for you if I were a spy?"

"Who brought Trovic into this office for the first time? Did you?"

"No. Mr. Glover met him outside. I do not know how or where."

"But afterwards you were friendly with Trovic?"

"Mr. Glover ordered me to keep in touch with him."

"And you became friendly?"

"Not friendly. I learned nothing about him, if that is what you mean. If you will pardon me, sir . . ."

"How did you keep in touch with him?" Burton interrupted impatiently.

"He had an address with a barber in the Alexis quarter. I'm sorry, sir. I must ask you . . ."

"Well?"

"To excuse me. My toothache is very bad."

Burton swore. "Then go to a dentist, for God's sake! Go now!"

After Sokolny had gone, Burton sat in the outer office and stared round the place gloomily. The bareness and the lack of equipment disgusted him. A couple of desks with typewriters, a couple of tin filing cabinets, a few chairs, shelves for newspapers, wire letter baskets, a lot of dust. No teletype machines to bring in the news, because somebody or other in the cock-eyed administration looked upon such things with suspicion. Or maybe there was not enough news to warrant the expense of installation by the official agency, Trad. The old pre-war system of delivering carbon flimsies by messenger was good enough for them.

Now the silence irritated him. He switched on the radio, but, in less than a minute switched it off again. He looked over some items that had come in from the Trad Agency, but could find nothing worth cabling to America. A wad arrived from the Propaganda Ministry: the full programme of events to mark the anniversary of the New Democracy. A scribbled note from Gregor came with it: "See me about your tickets."

To hell with the tickets!

His eyes kept straying towards the door. Every time a shadow fell across the glass panel, he would wait expectantly.

So the old man wanted to get her out of it. Get her to America, where she could marry and settle down to the proper business of a young woman.

Burton crushed a piece of spoiled paper and threw it into the wastebasket. Maybe he should marry her himself and see that she settled down to it. Then Burton, the old family man, could come home to embroidered slippers and a seat by the fireside. He stared distastefully at the Propaganda Ministry's programme.

"The revered head of the State, President Riecke, will arrive at the North Station at 10 A.M. punctually."

Punctually? Good for President Riecke! Three cheers for President Riecke!

He picked up Anna's phone and asked for a number.

"Settembrini?" he inquired. "This is Burton. I want to see you . . . After lunch? . . . Fine."

The Italian was usually a source of information. He knew everybody and everything, but nobody seemed to know much about him, except that he had come to the country about thirty years ago, had married, settled down, and built up a business as a photographer. Previously he must have travelled a great deal. He was a man of culture, a linguist, a wit of sorts. He had brought an independent mind unblemished through wars and political turmoil, and, under the new regime, he went on taking photographs of people and places with official sanction. The Propaganda Ministry found him invaluable. Settembrini could produce tougher proletarians against more dramatic cloud effects than any other photographer in the business, and his portraits of government notabilities had been published round the world. Burton had always found him a lively commentator. He went to the appointment eagerly.

"Maras?" Settembrini considered. "One of the old-school liberals. It's a little difficult to put the right political label on him. Before the war he might have been described as a radical Social Democrat, except that he hated the Social Democrats. The war simplified things. You were of the Resistance, or you co-operated. Maras and Riecke were associated in working against the invader. They were active in underground journalism; they were said to be the brains of the Resistance, but myself I doubt if there is a milligram of cerebral matter in the revered President's head."

"Yet he is the President?"

"By virtue of a push at the right time in the right direction. Maras was possibly the strong man of the Resistance. He might have been the leader after the Liberation, but his inclinations were towards the West. For the professor of modern history, the pasty glitter of an earlier freedom, the Napoleonic constitution, outshone the figure of Karl Marx. The professor was out of date. Riecke was pushed into the job. An ideal man, Burton. Gentle, benevolent, fond of children. And beautifully constructed. There is no hint of the mechanism when the strings are pulled. The action of the jaw conveys an impression of independent movement. He had always talked vaguely of a beautiful Utopia with shepherds piping and maidens dancing. He thinks he has it. I imagine they send the ballet up to his country estate occasionally to stage a pastoral scene. Just to confirm him in the illusion. Daphnis and Chloe to something a little more primitive than Ravel. An oboe and an ocarina, perhaps. I hope he doesn't recognise any of his shepherdesses when he is conveyed to the opera next week."

"I came to you to get away from myths," Burton complained.

"You haven't travelled far enough, my friend." Settembrini grinned. "You'll need a change of climate."

"Let's go back to Maras."

"Maras. He's almost a myth in himself. I think most of him died when his son was murdered. That was a quite dreadful business. It knocked the heart out of the man. They tell me he's very sick these days and hasn't got long to live. He shuts himself up in a place somewhere outside the town."

"Tolnitz."

"That's it. The revered Riecke saw to it. Gave him a pension, had the house put at his disposal, commanded the best medical attention. Riecke always gets his own way in things that don't matter. It confirms him in his private view that he's a dictator. A decent old man. He quarrelled bitterly with Maras over his Utopia, but he's entirely without rancour. I don't know what he'll say when Maras publishes the book he's writing. Possibly it never will be published. There's a daughter to consider. You may offer yourself for martyrdom, but you don't necessarily consign your offspring to the pyre."

"What do you know about the book?"

"Nothing, but I can imagine a lot. It's to be a history of the State from the eighteenth century onward. He will set the background and then proceed to battle. From what I heard of his mood at the time of the great quarrel, I judge he will demolish our New Democracy. We'll all be left choking in the dust of the temple."

But the daughter would be out of it, residing with an aunt in Boston, or married to some sucker of a newspaper man. In due course, no doubt, the newspaper man would be invited to smuggle a manuscript as well as the daughter out of the country. The book would make quite a sensation in America. Possibly the daughter would too. It was quite a beautiful scheme.

Settembrini said, "Funny, when you come to think of it. Riecke will have to sign the death warrant. And he'll be powerless to help the girl, though possibly she won't need his help. She's clever, from all accounts. She was on the run for years and the Nazis couldn't catch up with her. She was just a child then, but she learned the whole technique. She might find it useful again if she's ever up against the present police system. Incidentally, I wonder what's become of her."

# XI

The bassoon notes of Mr. Sesnik sounded persuasively from the inner office. They were sympathetic, condoling, full of reedy understanding. He too had suffered in his day, but now that Sokolny had had the offending molars removed, all the trouble would soon be over. The bassoon notes rose cheerfully. You had the impression that Mr. Sesnik was waiting expectantly for the sunrise.

Burton swore under his breath. He slammed the outer door and strode into his room. Sesnik had crawled out from under his stone and was seated at *his,* Burton's, desk, in *his,* Burton's, chair. Next thing he'd be going through the desk, if he hadn't been through it already.

Sesnik hauled himself from the chair. "My dear friend," he said. "I have been waiting to see you."

"If you had telephoned for an appointment, I wouldn't have kept you waiting."

"Don't apologise, Mr. Burton. I was passing. I paid a friendly call. Nothing formal. Nothing important. Actually I was out shopping." He indicated a rectangular parcel on the desk. "Sokolny has been telling me about his teeth, poor fellow."

Sokolny had a white wax look. He held one hand to his jaw. "It is always something of a shock." Sesnik was deeply concerned. "I think you ought to let the poor fellow go home. Three extractions, and one of them quite painful." He turned to the sufferer. "You should have gone to my dentist, Sokolny. If you had asked me, I could have fixed it."

Burton suddenly lost his temper. "You fix too many things already, my friend," he snapped.

"Please?" Sesnik's eyebrows met his scalp with amazement.

"Things like fixing to have me followed around town as if I were some kind of cheap crook, for instance. You'd better get this straight: if I have any more of it, I'll make a formal complaint."

"But my dear Mr. Burton! You are entirely mistaken."

"What sort of half wit do you think I am? You had a man on my tail yesterday. This morning another one is waiting for me outside my hotel. He followed me to lunch. He followed ]me too on a visit to Settembrini, the photographer. He followed me back here. He's down in the street right now, watching the door of the building."

"I beg you to pause before you reflect on my department, Mr. Burton. I would not like you to make a formal complaint before I conduct a thorough investigation."

The deep voice was soothing; there was no overtone of sarcasm to point to the fatuity of Burton's threat. Mr. Sesnik was a good friend, determined not to take offence over a foolish misunderstanding. He waddled to the window and leaned forward over his own facade.

"Show me the man," he pleaded.

Following the snow flurry of the morning, the afternoon was bright and clear. Burton looked, but the man was not in sight. He was attracted by a figure in a doorway fifty yards away. He peered, shook his head. "No," he said. "I don't see him now. I've no doubt he's waiting all the same."

"This gives me much concern, my friend." Sesnik frowned. "Through no fault of your own, you have become involved with criminals, dangerous criminals."

Burton stared. He was thinking about that figure in the doorway down the street, trying to place the man.

Someone, a messenger, opened the door of the outer office, and Sokolny took the opportunity to make an exit. Burton followed him to the communicating door and closed it.

He said, "Because I was tricked by this Trovic, I am involved with his gang. If that's what you mean, it doesn't make sense. Trovic has got away. Why should the rest of them worry about me?"

The round moonface of Mr. Sesnik smiled sadly. "You are not yet fully acclimated, my dear friend. For that reason we must exercise every precaution. These criminals are aware that you and I have become acquainted. They say to themselves, 'Why is that old fox Sesnik cultivating the American?' And the answer they arrive at is disturbing. They begin to wonder how much you know, how much Trovic betrayed to you, how much you will betray to the old fox. What you must realise is this: among these scum, betrayal is in the air, and their fine Trovic has bolted, helped by the American who is so friendly with the cunning Sesnik. That is why I am concerned, Mr. Burton. I am the more concerned, because I am in a measure responsible."

It was ingenious balderdash. It might even have been convincing if Trovic had really bolted; convincing enough to throw a scare into a man who was very unsure of himself.

"I see." Burton realised that it was polite to swallow the story. The small eyes were fixed upon his; the button nose and the gentle comical mouth contributed to an expression of benevolent concern. Burton looked away. For the first time he did feel unsure of himself. He was in it now. He had knowledge of Trovic that Sesnik lacked, and that alone was enough. There could be no more protestations of righteous indignation from the innocent foreign correspondent. Sesnik was justified in having him shadowed; whatever Sesnik might do, he would be justified. The only way out for the innocent correspondent was to tell Sesnik what he knew. Betrayal was in the air, part of the political climate.

Burton repressed a grin.

Sesnik said, "Don't worry about it. I will put a man on to watch the man who is shadowing you. I give you my personal guarantee, no harm will come to you."

"I hope I'm not going to be followed for the whole of my stay here."

"No, no! We will arrest the shadow. That will be the end of it. The others will be frightened."

Burton felt his face becoming unnaturally solemn. The grin was getting more difficult to repress.

"I mustn't take up more of your time." The moonface smiled amiably. "Actually, I called in merely to see Miss Maras, a personal matter. Sokolny tells me she has been away for two days. I trust it is not sickness."

"Her father had an attack. She has been with him at Tolnitz."

"Too bad." The bassoon cooed. "I'm afraid the old man is not long for this world."

"I believe he got over it all right. I told her not to hurry back but I'm hoping she will. We'll be having a busy time next week, with all the festivities."

"That reminds me. If you are not satisfied with your seat allocation for the parade, do let me know. I will fix it."

"Thanks. Aren't you forgetting your parcel?"

"So I am." Sesnik revolved on his small shining shoes, picked up the package, stripped the wrapping away, and revealed a large, gaily coloured box. "Chocolates for Anna," he explained. "Shall I leave them on her desk?"

He waddled into the outer office. Sokolny sprang up and attended his departure, accompanying him along the corridor. Burton looked to see what the messenger had brought. There were a mimeographed departmental report and a couple of flimsies from the Trad Agency on Sokolny's desk. Beside them lay a sealed envelope marked confidential and addressed in spidery printing to Charles J. Burton. He opened it incuriously and a slip of pasteboard fell from it.

A ticket for the opera, Box B, Seat Four, Grand Tier. For that night's performance.

The press tickets usually came in pairs, but this was definitely no press ticket. Burton retrieved the envelope from the wastebasket and turned it over. A faint whiff of scent made him think of Babette. It was her perfume, or did he associate the ticket with her because she was the only person he knew at the Opera House.

He looked at the programme on the wall. The bill for the night was *Prince Igor.*

It checked up. Babette would be one of the maidens in the Polovtsian dances.

When Sokolny came back Burton showed him the torn envelope.

"Who delivered this?" he demanded.

Sokolny started to shake his head, but the movement made him grimace with pain. "I don't know," he said. "It was dropped through the flap."

"When?"

"While you were talking to Mr. Sesnik."

"All right," Burton told him. "You'd better get along home. I'll attend to things."

Sokolny's suffering eyes were full of gratitude. He buttoned up his worn coat and went.

Burton stood with the ticket in his hand.

The opera!

An idea sent him swiftly to the window of the inner office. The man he had seen in the doorway fifty yards down the street was still there. He seemed not to have moved at all. He had a cigarette in his mouth and was reading a newspaper.

The suggestion of familiarity was explained. The ticket had given Burton the cue. The lounger was the man who had hustled Anna Maras from the stage door of the Opera House and driven off with her in the battered car.

Burton took his binoculars from a drawer and focused them. He was quite sure then about the identity of the man, and it required no leap of the imagination to associate him with Trovic.

The thought was disquieting. It lent credibility to a suggestion he had dismissed as a deliberate fantasy of Sesnik's. He was shaken, but he could still argue that it was nonsense to suppose that Trovic would have him watched.

He lowered the binoculars. Sokolny came into view, proceeding along the same side of the street on his way home, taking jerky, loping strides that made him look like some obscene insect.

The lounger saw him coming and drew back into the doorway, out of sight. Sokolny passed. The young man reappeared, waited a few seconds, then started along the street in Sokolny's wake.

Burton raised his binoculars and followed the course of the pair. All the way down the street the young man kept about twenty-five yards behind the other. Sokolny never looked back. At the Alexis Bridge he waited for his bus. The young man closed up the gap and loitered near the stopping point. When the bus came along Sokolny was standing near the head of the line. The young man pressed forward and managed to scramble on board.

# XII

The box attendant on the Grand Tier scrutinised the ticket carefully, then spoke in French, keeping his voice low. "You are M'sieu Burton, are you not?" Waiting for confirmation, he made the seat holder the object of another careful scrutiny. Then he led the way along the curving red-carpeted corridor and opened the door of the box. A man and two young women had already occupied the three chairs along the balustrade. They paid no attention to the newcomer. It was the custom to fill all the seats in the boxes.

"This is your chair, m'sieu," the attendant said. "If I can find you a better place, I will come for you after the curtain rises." He glanced at the backs of the three occupants, then at Burton with a curious smile and a slight shrug that said in effect, "I don't think they understand French, anyway."

Burton nodded. It was getting beyond him, but he showed no surprise. It was his part to take everything as a matter of course, even if they asked him to conduct the opera. There had been moments during the evening when he had thought that he was walking into some kind of trap. It was all so mysterious; melodramatic in the style of Sardou; as Gothic as the spires on the Police Judiciary. He felt he needed a cloak to swathe him and hide his face. He had felt the need particularly as he had repeated the rear-door escape from his hotel. Now, divested of his commonplace hat and coat, he was singularly defenceless.

The man in front of him turned with a comradely smile. "Your seat is not good," he observed. "Perhaps we can make room."

"No, thank you." Burton sought another expression from his mental phrase book. "I am all right." The impossibility of making room was manifest. The comradely young man went into a long harangue. Probably he was criticising the design of the opera house as something hopelessly bourgeois, not adapted to the new rule of equality and freedom. Burton did not know. It was all beyond the phrase book. The young man rose, then Burton understood with dismay that he was offering to change places. One of the ladies exhibited disapproval. Burton tried some more of his vocabulary. A better seat would be found for him. In any case he merely wished to hear the music. Fingers plucked at the young man's sleeve, the lights began to dim, the situation was saved.

When the curtain went up Burton made no effort to see the stage. He was not interested. He liked Borodin, but tonight was no time to listen to music. He sat back in the box, waiting, involved in a plot more intricate than the wars of Prince Igor against the Polovtsi. He had not long to wait. In a sustained fortissimo from the orchestra the opening of the box door was unheard. The attendant tapped him on the shoulder, and he rose.

"This way, m'sieu."

He was more conscious now of the music. A baritone voice rose in a fine phrase as he walked along the corridor to its end. The attendant drew back a plush curtain and pushed open the heavy fireproof pass door. At the same instant he glanced back cautiously, but there was no one in the curving corridor.

"Quickly, m'sieu."

Burton entered the dim-lit passage, and the door thudded behind him. Babette was there, slender in a cotton wrap, but with face transformed into the wild beauty of a Polovtsian girl.

"Follow me." She touched his hand, then went swiftly on ahead of him, down a short flight of stairs. Here, there was a long passage with doors, and now the music was far away. At the end of the passage Babette opened a door, and Burton saw Anna Maras.

"I will come back for you, m'sieu," Babette said.

Anna closed the door, shutting out all sound.

She said, "I hope you will forgive me. I heard from Babette of the trouble you have taken, or I would not have dared to bring you here."

He wanted to hold her, to communicate by touch the relief he felt at seeing her. He wished to say how anxious he had been and how glad he was that she was safe. Instead, he asked her a question that must have seemed querulous at least.

"Is it necessary to take all these precautions?"

"We know you have been watched," she answered. "We learned during the Resistance that we could not be too careful. We had to make sure that you were not followed."

We, we, we! Relief in him gave way to something like bitterness. "So you were working with Trovic all the time," he said. "You knew what he was doing."

"No," she answered. "I knew nothing until Sesnik telephoned. Then I became anxious for some of my friends; for my father and myself. There were things I had to do. I wished to return to you at the ballet, but it became impossible. When I saw you coming to look for me, I wanted to speak to you. It was the wrong thing. There was too much urgency then."

"What are you going to do now? You can't go on hiding yourself."

"I don't think it's necessary. I have done nothing that Sesnik knows of. You have talked with him again. That's why I needed to see you. He has not arrested Sokolny?"

"Not up to five o'clock."

"That is all right, then. Sokolny has said nothing."

"What could he say? Does he know anything? Why should Sesnik arrest him?"

"Sesnik is suspicious of everyone. I don't know what information Sokolny has. I know so little of anything. I've been out of it. You must believe that." She was earnest in pleading, watching Burton anxiously. "Do you think Sesnik really believes that Trovic has escaped?"

"Yes. He's quite at sea over it. Confused, I mean."

"He's never confused," Anna asserted. "He may sometimes be very wrong. Always he is cunning."

Burton heard a roll of timpani muted by the walls. It had the sound of very distant thunder. The room was a cubby-hole like the one in which he had interviewed Babette. A battered roll-top desk was stacked with dusty papers. Scores and libretto books lay in disarray and some rough sketches of scenery added to the litter. One of the sketches had fallen to the floor. It looked like a design for the Kremlin scene in *Boris*. It was defaced by an enormous ink blot.

"Sesnik came to see you today," Burton said. "I told him that your father had had an attack and that you were at Tolnitz with my permission. If he investigates tonight, he may discover that you haven't been there."

"My father will know what to say." Anna was calmly confident. "If Sesnik investigates tomorrow, I shall be there. I am going to Tolnitz when I leave here. I want you to spare me for another day. Please."

"Then you *will* return to the office?" He said it too eagerly, unable to keep the relief out of his voice. He would not admit it; he might deny it with a bitter show of words, but he wanted her beside him under any conditions.

She said, "I shall be back at my lodging tomorrow night if nothing happens to Sokolny. That is the important thing, the" —she hesitated—"the point of danger. Sokolny. How shall I know if he is still free?"

"There's no difficulty about that," he decided. "I'll hire a car and come to Tolnitz for you."

She shook her head. "You must keep out of it." "It's too late to tell me that." Burton laughed. "I'm in quite deeply. I don't like being made a fool of. Anything else is okay."

She reached for his hand and gripped it tightly for an instant.

Then, as suddenly, she withdrew her hand and looked up at him almost as if something had startled her. He frowned and, turning away, picked up the sketch from the floor. He had been right about it. There was a scrawl under the drawing. "Boris Godounov, Prologue, Sc. II."

He remembered how fond she was of Moussorgsky, and it annoyed him at that moment to remember anything of her likes and dislikes.

"Don't go getting any wrong ideas about me," he said. "I'm not joining your movement, whatever it is. I'm a newspaper man. You ought to know what that is by now. Whatever I do, I do for reward. There's a story in this business somewhere, and maybe I'll dig it out. I've a feeling it could be something bigger than a horse fair."

"If I could give you a story, I would," she answered. "There's nothing I can say."

He put the sketch down on the desk.

"Who is this Trovic? What sort of game is he playing?"

Then it came out, though he had wanted to hold it back.

"What's he *to you?*"

She stared at him dumbly and it might have been appealingly. He waited a moment. They were shut away in silence. The only thing that penetrated was the distant rumble of timpani.

"All right," he said. "Forget it."

"I thought there would be no more of this for me, or I would never have taken work with you," she told him. "I will resign when it becomes possible. For the time, I must return. Also I must ask your help. I will telephone you late tomorrow afternoon. I will inquire how you are, and if you say very well, I will understand that Sokolny is safe. Then I will take the bus to town. It will be necessary to be careful on the telephone. The police may be listening."

"Careful, sure!" He met her gaze again. "We'll keep everything aboveboard. You will not ask how I am. You will say you are ready to return and I'll inform you that I'm coming to Tolnitz."

She tried to argue that there was no need for him to make the trip, but he ignored her protest. "I'll tell you about Sokolny when I see you," he added.

"Babette will be coming soon." She paused. "I think Sokolny will be all right. I spoke to him before Sesnik saw him. I will speak to him again. He is very nervous and easily frightened, but he will be safe enough unless they drag him in and put him under pressure."

She looked at the watch on her wrist.

"Should you be on the way to Tolnitz?" he asked.

"It's not that." She opened the door and listened to the faint sounds from the orchestra. "We've had to time everything carefully. I don't know exactly where they are in the score. You are to go back through the pass door just before the fall of the curtain. At that moment there will be no one in the passage. Babette and I have friends here, but not everyone is a friend."

She continued to listen with the door ajar. "I should be more familiar with Prince Igor," she said.

"Do you know that I went to Tolnitz last night?" He was at the roll-top desk, looking at the scene sketches.

"Tolnitz!" She spoke in alarm.

"I wasn't followed," he assured her. "I was careful to see to that."

She closed the door and moved towards him. "What happened?" she demanded.

He gave her an account of his visit. "I like your father," he said. "He's a good man. He's very anxious about your future."

"That's not exceptional. We are all anxious about our futures."

"Anna, you were happy in America. .. ."

"I was a child. I have lived since then."

"If I could get you out of this country, would you again be happy in America?"

She hesitated. There was that to it. She said, "My happiness is unimportant."

"That's a dumb remark. Would you go if it could be arranged?"

"No." There was no hesitation this time. "Do you think I could leave my father?"

"If he wishes it. . . ."

The door was thrown open and Babette was there in the gay barbaric colours of her Polovtsi skirts.

"Quickly!" she whispered, and Anna hustled him through the door.

Babette moved swiftly along in front of him, her bangles jingling faintly. He followed her up the stairs and almost cannoned into her when she halted suddenly on the top step and wildly motioned him to retreat.

They were cut off from the pass door. Someone who must not see him was in the passage.

"This way!"

He was conscious of mounting sound from orchestra and stage. The climax was near.

Babette hauled him along another passage, took an abrupt turning, and unlocked a door. It was a stubborn door. She tugged in vain at the handle, then made way for him to try. The barrier yielded suddenly. She pushed him through the opening and closed the door after him.

The impact of cold night air made him gasp. He was standing on a balustraded platform near the rear of the great theatre. Without hat or coat to shield him, he felt the piercing thrust of a rising wind from across the Dreva. He hurried down the steps to the pavement and turned towards the front of the house. In Opera Place he caught the full blast of the wind. He shivered as he climbed the steps to the lighted colonnade. There had been none to see him in the side street, and now the interval had been reached. The doors were swinging open. A few of the audience emerged to sample the air. Burton mingled with them and entered the foyer. He did not go back to the Grand Tier. Instead he took his hat and coat from the cloakroom and left the building.

He knew that Anna Maras would be making her own way to Tolnitz and that he must keep away from her. Then, turning over in his mind the things she had said, he began to worry about Sokolny. He saw Sokolny shifting from one foot to another, teetering between loyalty and treachery. The image might be without validity, but Burton wanted to rid himself of it. He needed company, needed to relax. Attridge might be at the Metropole, or Dick Trask. Even Mervan would do if no one else offered.

The bar was pretty full: the usual bunch of army officers and airmen, a sprinkling of the superior civil servants, some distinguished visitors from across the eastern frontiers, some local engineers, women at the tables. Not a newspaper man in sight.

Burton ordered some of the wretched whisky and took it to a table. Then he saw company approaching, but it was not of the kind he craved. Mr. Sesnik waddled forward on gleaming footwear. The moonface beamed a greeting, then assumed a rather comical expression of concern.

"My dear friend!" Sesnik's fat hand descended affectionately on Burton's shoulder. "I am relieved to see you. Perhaps you will help me in my little dilemma. I am having some trouble with your poor Sokolny."

"Sokolny!" Burton spilled some of his whisky. "He is over in that corner. I'm afraid he has had too much to drink. Just a trifle too much."

Burton followed Sesnik down the length of the bar. The fat man's face was all concern.

"You must not be severe on the poor fellow," he pleaded. "It is a terrible thing to have three teeth out in one day. Perhaps he should not have drunk alcohol, but in the circumstances a lapse is understandable. It seems that the pain is a long time in passing. He wished to ease it."

Sokolny had passed out across the table.

Sesnik explained: "We were having a few drinks, and quite suddenly he was out of control. I was about to call for the assistance of a waiter when I saw you enter. I think we ought to get him into a cab and take him home."

Burton lifted Sokolny by the shoulders and shook him. The man opened his eyes, stared owlishly, and began to mutter and mumble. Burton caught the name of Trovic.

"What about Trovic?" he demanded sharply.

"Nothing about. Know nothing." Sokolny rocked dizzily. "Ask Glover."

"What the hell have you been trying to do?" Burton snapped at Sesnik.

"Now, now, Mr. Burton!" The bassoon sounded a key of quiet reproof. "The poor fellow doesn't know what he is saying. Perhaps you yourself were asking him about Trovic at some time. You must not leap at conclusions, my dear friend. We are making enough of a spectacle as it is."

Burton signalled to a waiter and together they got Sokolny into a cab, with Sesnik waddling behind them like an anxious shepherd, ready to give the address to the driver, even prepared to see the unfortunate sufferer to his room. "It is my duty," the fat man said. "I feel partly responsible."

"Too bad," Burton told him. "I'll take over from here, so you can stop worrying." A young man stood among the curious spectators on the pavement behind Sesnik. Burton peered through the window as the cab moved from the curb. The young man was the lounger who had followed Sokolny to the Alexis Bridge and boarded the same bus.

# XIII

Sesnik staged his comedy of the shadowers quite early next day. Burton left his hotel without bothering about the inevitable watcher. He had forgotten Sesnik's promise of intervention, but was soon reminded of it by an altercation behind him. He turned and saw one plain-clothes man struggling with another, while pedestrians came running to see what was going on. The supposed culprit was handcuffed by his colleague and led forward for Burton's inspection.

"Is he der criminale who follow you after, yes?"

Sesnik had had the courtesy to provide an actor with an elementary knowledge of English.

Burton shook his head. "Perhaps. I don't know. I can't remember having seen him before."

"It is heem," the captor insisted. "I watch. He wait outside hotel. You come. He follow you after. Okay?"

"What do you want me to do? Go with you?"

"No, no! I make reports to Commissioner Sesnik. No more you have the trouble from spyings. That is all."

All except that now there would be a more subtle talent on the job! But Burton no longer cared. He intended to keep his movements in the open. If the need came for further clandestine action, he would have to be doubly careful.

Sokolny was late for work, but the night out seemed to have done him good. He was less nervous, more cheerful. He announced that he was feeling much better.

"I'm sorry about last night," he said. "I must have given you a lot of trouble. I owe you much gratitude for what you did."

"That's all right." Burton regarded him bleakly. "What started you? Did Sesnik pick you up?"

"Indeed, no. I met Monsieur Mervan. He took me to the Metropole and bought me a drink. Mr. Sesnik came in later and joined us.

He was oscillating from foot to foot at such an alarming rate that Burton told him to sit down.

Seated, Sokolny fingered his collar, but his Adam's apple had plenty of room. He said, "I had the wrong impression about Sesnik. He is a nice man. A very nice man. He likes you. Mr. Glover he did not like, but he likes you. He says if all the foreign correspondents were of your type, there would be no more trouble."

"And you think that's a compliment?" Burton put quite a snarl into it. "How many drinks did he buy you?"

Sokolny's gaze faltered. He looked down at the desk. "You must understand, sir, it was just a friendly occasion, a meeting by accident."

"Sure, I understand. He filled you full of liquor and then tried to pump you. The mistake he made was that he gave you one shot too many. You passed out cold on him."

"I do not remember."

"Do you remember if you told him anything? He asked you about Trovic, didn't he?"

"But I know nothing of Trovic." Sokolny turned his eyes towards the window. "I only knew him as the man Mr. Glover employed."

"All right. Get this in your head. Any information about what happens in this office comes from me. If people ask you questions, you refer them to me. It doesn't matter what the subject may be, Trovic or anything else. You don't know a thing. That's a matter of office policy. Understand?" "That is what I've always understood. All the same, Mr. Burton, I think you are misjudging Sesnik."

"I don't think I could. Now forget Sesnik and listen to me. I want to find out some more about this new escape project."

"It is impossible, sir. The people behind it will know that Sesnik has been here. I have been warned. It is too dangerous for anyone to say anything now."

"Has Trovic anything to do with it?"

"Trovic is out of the country."

"That's no reply to my question."

"Trovic knew nothing about it. He has employed the organisation, but is not of it."

"The organisation? So it is the Universal Travel Agency?"

He used the label devised by the foreign-press colony. "Answer me, Sokolny! Is it the U.T.A.?"

"I did not say so." Sokolny had an attack of nerves again. His eyes shifted furtively from one object to another in the room. "You must not ask me these questions," he protested.

"I'll ask you all the questions I need to. If you want to keep your job, you'll answer them."

Sokolny pleaded. He had always been a loyal servant. He had taken great risks. He had done so many things that were not permitted.

"Too many," Burton said. "You've got me in a mess with the police, you and Trovic. And don't talk to me about Mr. Glover. I know all about that; more than you think. I know that Glover arranged to get a man out of the country, and you helped him."

"It is untrue. I did nothing."

"We'll see. I'm not going to sit back and be penalised for what you and Glover did." Burton reached across the desk for the telephone. "If you won't confide in me, I'm going to do something you won't like." "What are you doing?" Sokolny was in a panic.

"Calling Sesnik. We'll have him come round for another little talk. Maybe he'll throw some light on things when I tell him what I know." Burton watched the frightened man. "Well?" he demanded. "Do I call or do you talk?"

He was thinking, while he waited, that it was a painfully transparent bluff, but it worked.

"What do you wish to know?" Sokolny asked miserably.

"Are you an agent of the U.T.A.?"

"No."

"How can I get in touch with them?"

"I cannot tell you that. I cannot."

"Quit fooling, Sokolny. You must make up your mind whose side you are on. I want to know the name of an agent. It will be just as safe with me as it is with you."

"I don't know any agent. I have a friend. That is all. Perhaps he has another friend. I am not sure. No one is ever sure. That is how it works."

"I give you my word, I'll cause no trouble for your friend."

"No. I will see him. I'll find out if there is any more news."

Burton pulled the phone towards him again. "I don't want news. I want the man's name."

Sokolny writhed, moaning under a weight of misfortune.

"What's the matter?" Burton asked. "Is it your jaw again?"

It was a worse torture, but he would not break under it. He held his head in his hands and strove in misery. Perhaps he thought there would be no betrayal if he found the right formula. A denial, followed by a simple assertion . . .

"I misled you," he said at last. "I have no friend. You will remember that I have told you nothing. I have nothing to tell."

"What is this nonsense?" Burton asked harshly.

"It is not nonsense." Sokolny struggled to assume a thin dignity. "I have been thinking. If a watch should need re-pairs, there is a good man on the Breclin Quay, four doors from the Alexis Bridge. The name is Dovinye, Emil Dovinye. He speaks French but no English."

Burton stared at Sokolny, wondering. He was getting acclimated fast, but the involutions of the native mind still seemed a little peculiar. At first he was full of contempt for Sokolny; then he felt the anxiety that Anna had expressed. Sokolny was unsafe. It was so simple a matter to commend the watchmaker of the Breclin Quay to Sesnik or anybody else. Obviously Sokolny had held out against Sesnik so far, but if Sesnik pulled him in and took him to the Judiciary building, fear would be played against fear until he gave in.

Fear was real enough in him and no ingenious balm of words could soften it for long. In a moment it was pricking him again. He shifted in his chair, then got on to his feet.

"I would not have told you," he said, "but I know you are to be trusted. As it is, I will be responsible as your guarantor." The thin dignity was holding, but the pale wedge face had gone paler and the man's hands were trembling. "If anything happens, I will be a hostage."

"Nothing terrible will happen as long as you don't talk to Sesnik."

"I'll never do that. They would kill me. Sesnik is interested only in Trovic. He believes I know nothing about Trovic. He blames Mr. Glover for everything. Sesnik is a good fellow, except when he suspects. It is you who must be careful, Mr. Burton. He suspects you because of Glover."

"Don't worry about me," Burton told him. "I can look after myself. I can look after you, too, if you don't make a fool of yourself."

Sokolny started to say something, but checked and left it to his pleading eyes.

"All right," Burton assured him. "What do I do to get to see Dovinye; just walk into the shop and say how do?" "No. It will be necessary to take my watch to him." Sokolny began to undo the buckle of the wristband. "One moment, I will give it to you."

Burton stopped him. "Leave it," he said. "I'll borrow it when I need it."

# XIV

Sesnik telephoned to communicate the imaginary result of the bogus arrest. "It is just as I thought, my dear Burton," he said. "The man who was following you was one of the Trovic gang. He has confessed."

"I hope you didn't have to torture him," Burton responded with a pretence of anxiety. "He looked a half-witted sort of clod."

Sesnik laughed so heartily that the receiver crackled with the noise of it. "We are a little more refined, my dear fellow. One of these days I will invite you round to witness our methods. You will be surprised at the effect of gentleness on the most stubborn mind."

"Let's make a date after the festivities. Did you learn any more about Trovic?"

"Unfortunately, no. The prisoner is just a supernumerary. He was not in the counsels of the higher-ups. He knew nothing at all. He had orders to report on your movements."

"To whom?"

"That he has not yet disclosed. We will take care of it in due course. The important thing is that we have rid you of a nuisance."

"It's very good of you."

"Not at all. I am most happy if I have been of service. I don't think you will have any more trouble. If you do, just telephone me at once." "Thanks, but it's not so important. After all, there's no secrecy about my movements. I don't really care who sees them."

"Of course not, my dear Burton. It is quite absurd, but that is the way these types behave. Is there any news of Anna Maras, by the way?"

"Not yet. I suppose she's still out at Tolnitz. You're not anxious about her, are you?"

"Certainly not."

"You sounded as if you were. If you should run out to Tolnitz, let me know if she is all right. As she isn't on the telephone out there, I have to wait for her to call me. I expect she'll be back at work pretty soon."

"Well, give her my chocolates, won't you? Does Sokolny feel ill this morning?"

"Very ill. Full of remorse."

Sesnik laughed heartily again. Sokolny was an amusing fellow, so naive. A cheerful note to end the call.

Burton took Sokolny out to lunch. If he could, he would see that there was no future interference with the man before he had another talk with Anna.

She telephoned at five o'clock and it was arranged that he should pick her up at seven. A few minutes after he put down the receiver, a messenger arrived with a report from the Ministry of Planning. It was without warning. It had not been expected for several days yet. It was important. It had to be dealt with at once and it was of a formidable size.

He scanned the brief description supplied in English, then handed the mass of mimeographed paper to Sokolny.

"You'll have to work late," he said. "Make an extract of the general statistics and then pick out the principal points in the section on engineering. That's what we're interested in. Don't fuss about your English. I'll bring Anna in to check. Between the three of us we'll get a cable away tonight. The rest of the stuff can be dealt with tomorrow." He went to his desk, but returned to Sokolny with an afterthought. "Lock the outer door when I've gone. I don't want to have you interrupted."

The sky at dusk looked heavy with a threat of snow, but Burton judged that he could be back in town with Anna before a storm developed. He picked up an autocab a few yards from the office building. He turned several times to peer through the rear window, but saw nothing to suggest that he was being followed until his vehicle was well clear of the city; then he noticed that a car behind him was keeping a distance of three hundred yards or so. Others overtook and passed the autocab, but that one car was content with its comfortable pace. Sesnik was a persistent fellow; but after all it was his job to be persistent.

With Tolnitz in sight Burton took one more glance at the car and then forgot about it. He was in a cheerful mood, almost elated, as he gave the driver directions for finding the house.

"Stop at the first gate," he said.

Tonight there was light in more than one room, but the jalousies were still closed over the windows.

Anna met him before he had gone half way up the ruined path.

"I heard the car," she explained. "I thought I would save time. I have no baggage."

"Do I see your father?"

"It is not necessary. He is, in fact, engaged with a friend, and asks me to give you greetings."

"Is he well?"

"Yes. He is very well. Shall we go?"

It seemed to him that she was eager to get him away from the house, but soon he put it out of his head. She seemed happy, in a mood to match his own mood. She had shed most, if not all, of the anxiety he had seen in her the previous night, and when he told her about Sokolny she was confident that everything would be all right.

"I will speak with him," she said, as if that would determine the problem. There was a hardness in her voice that made him turn, but he could see her only faintly in the interior of the cab.

A pair of lights moved in a byway and swung into the main road behind them. He was amused by Sesnik's limpet-like devotion. He remarked on it to Anna and described the act put on by the two police comedians that morning. "They should be at the National Theatre," he commented. "One of them is probably in that car behind us."

Anna smiled. "I know that you take all precautions," she said. "It is Sokolny I have been worrying about. No doubt they have been watching him too."

"One of your friends has, at any rate."

"One of my friends?" Her voice was sharp, rising to anxiety.

He related what he had seen from the window of the office the previous night.

She was silent for so long that he asked her what was the matter.

"I must see Sokolny tonight," she answered. "I hope he is not wandering about the city again."

"He's safe at the office, working hard." He told her why, and what he had arranged. "I'd like you to come in for a few minutes and check his translation. Afterwards I'll take you out to dine. I must make the deadline with a cable."

All her cheerfulness had gone. She was worrying again. Their arms were touching as they sat side by side in the cab, but she was remote from him, an isolate in some hard world of her own. When he tried to reassure her about Sokolny, she gave no sign that she had heard him.

Snow was falling when they reached the outer suburbs and soon it was coming down heavily. They were held up at a level crossing while a freight train panted and clanked towards the marshalling yards in the wide eastern loop of the Dreva. Anna shivered. It was cold in the cab. The heater wasn't working properly. On and on the train dragged, stopped, heaved back with a tremendous rattle of chains and a banging of bumpers, went forward again with more noise.

Burton slid back the glass panel. "Why do we get no heat?" he asked.

The driver did not understand. Anna repeated the question more correctly; the man became voluble.

"Suddenly the thing has broken," she translated. "He doesn't know how to fix it. If you are thinking of me, I am all right. It is not far now."

Her words were a rejection, as if his protest had been an unwanted approach to her. She drew away from him into her corner of the seat, making herself more remote. Mentally, he shrugged.

They were moving again, and he peered forward through the panel and the windscreen, seeing the street lights through a blur of snowflakes.

The bridge at last. The Dreva was a black lane between white banks. The cab skidded, recovered, and shot on. The traffic was light. The few pedestrians were hurrying, bodies bent forward.

Burton looked at his watch. Eight-thirty! He was thinking of the job again, noting that there was plenty of time.

The cab pulled up. He hurried Anna across the pavement and returned to pay the driver, his shoes crunching the snow.

It was warm in the vestibule. The janitor looked out of his cubicle and said good evening.

Anna was waiting at the foot of the stairs. She was the respectful secretary again, serious, but quite composed. She might never have been away from the office.

When they reached the door, he knocked. If Sokolny had followed instructions, he would have fixed the latch so it could be opened only from the inside.

He knocked a second time, then tried his key. It worked.

The lights were on in both offices, but Sokolny was not visible.

Burton hesitated on the threshold. An intimation of danger came to him. Suddenly the fear of what he might find was like a tangible obstacle in his path. He turned to glance at Anna, and, meeting her gaze, saw alarm in her eyes. They both knew that something had happened, as if the smell of disaster was in the air.

He remembered the anxiety she had expressed about Sokolny; her need to know that the man was safe, unmolested. He saw her lips move and heard her whisper the name.

"Sokolny?"

"He must have gone out to eat," Burton said.

"Someone has been here," Anna observed, pointing to the floor.

There were little pools and drops of water on the parquetry; melted snow from shoe welts or a hat brim. Someone had trudged through the storm, then hurried up the stairs. . . .

The planning report was on Sokolny's desk and a stack of copy paper showed that he had been busy on his translation.

Anna said, "It hasn't been snowing very long."

Burton crossed the room and halted in the doorway of the inner office.

Sokolny was there.

He was seated at the big desk with head and arms in a sprawl across the leatherette surface. The posture was ridiculously like that into which he had fallen at the Metropole, but this time he was not drunk. He was dead.

Burton was a step inside the room. He called sharply to Anna to keep out, but was too late. He wheeled and took hold of her, and she was trembling helplessly. He held her in his arms, and she clung tightly to him, pressing her face against him. He drew her into the outer office and closed the door behind him. He could still see all the details of the mess in sharp definition, but he had experienced that sort of thing before. The thing that worried him most at this moment was the effect of the shock on her. She continued to cling to him through spasms of shuddering; then by some effort of will she overcame the sickness.

"I'm all right now," she said. "I didn't think I could be so weak."

He made her sit in an armchair. He saw the chalky pallor of her face.

"I knew it would happen." She looked up with dread and sorrow in her eyes. "I wanted to save him. I wanted to. I told them ..."

She stood up suddenly and he pressed her to sit again. "Never mind now," he urged. "Stay where you are for a minute."

He went back into his office and took a bottle of whisky from a drawer of his desk. He poured a stiff glass and made the girl drain it. Then he picked up the telephone and called the Police Judiciary.

Sesnik was not in. Burton gave details to the man who answered for him and requested that Sesnik should be informed as soon as he could be reached. He wanted Sesnik, the one man he knew.

"The police will be there immediately," the official at the Judiciary told him. "Don't disturb anything. Just wait."

Burton put down the phone and crossed to the chair where Anna sat. He stood behind her and closed a hand on her right shoulder in a grip that was meant to be consoling.

"It is so cruel." She reached up to clasp his hand. "I hoped there would be no more of it. Now I can see only murder in their hearts. They can't be saved from themselves."

Burton did not ask her what she meant. He scarcely heard her words. He was thinking that whatever it was, this thing that had started, it would bring her into danger, and he had, somehow, to get her out of it.

He freed his hand from her grasp and once more returned to the inner office. He went to the desk, moving carefully, avoiding the revolver, which had fallen to the floor. He paused to listen, although he knew the police could not be here yet. There was silence, except for the mutter of snow against the panes of the window.

Then, he lifted Sokolny's left arm and took the watch from the wrist.

# XV

The place was overrun. Police in smart tunics and polished leggings marched up the stairs and along the corridor. They stood guard in the vestibule and on the landing and at the door of the outer office. But these were merely the chorus boys. They fell back before a cast of principals that included photographers, fingerprint experts, a surgeon, and several stern-faced investigators from the higher categories. The unimportant Sokolny was being vastly honoured in death. But for the continuing snowstorm, one might have expected to see comets blazing in the heavens.

Difficulties at once beset Burton. The police had brought along every kind of specialist except an interpreter, and the only foreign language any of them had was German. That was of no use to Burton. He did his best to answer them in their own tongue, but the result seemed of little use to them. When he suggested that Anna might interpret, they looked at him scornfully. What sort of fools did he think they were? They hurried Anna into the outer office and closed the door so that she would not hear what her accomplice said. It seemed obvious, from the grim, demanding tone of the incomprehensible questions, that they were satisfied about his guilt. Things became more confusing. When they howled at him, he roared back at them. What did they think he was going to do, confess to a murder of which he was entirely innocent? No, no, no, they said, and he took that to be a rejection of his claim.

"Bring Sesnik here," he insisted. "Sesnik, Sesnik, Sesnik!" he stormed. "No, no," they answered menacingly. "Jaffke." They kept on repeating that strange word, and Burton puzzled over it, but it turned out to be merely the name of their chief, and presently Jaffke arrived.

He was tall and lean and alert. He had the cunning calculating eyes of a Scarpia in the thin ascetic face of a Savonarola, but a Savonarola of a peculiarly Slavic cast. He listened to the underlings, gave himself up to profound thought, and came to a decision. All hung anxiously on his word. The moment was awesome. "Telephone for a man who speaks English," Jaffke commanded.

A hand reached for the instrument. Jaffke issued another command. Anna was brought in for interrogation.

"These fools can't understand anything," Burton complained to her. "Tell them--"

Several voices shouted at him, Jaffke made a small gesture, and Burton was marched into the outer office, where, through the closed door, he could hear the sounds of question and answer. He strained to catch a word, even a name, but nothing articulate came through the barrier, and he could judge only that Anna was quite controlled and that they were treating her with some courtesy.

He had time to think; but it was difficult to know what to think. He didn't yet know the real nature of his dilemma. Besides, the eyes of two uniformed guards were upon him all the time, distracting him, conveying the impression that they could read everything in his mind. He told himself it was absurd, that they were a couple of clods from the country, selected for the size of their muscles and trained to obey without reasoning. The illusion persisted. They could read his thoughts, and his thoughts were only of Anna and Sokolny's watch.

The murder of Sokolny was linked up with Trovic, and somehow Anna and Babette were in the chain. But if the police found Sokolny's wrist watch in his pocket, where would that place Anna? As his accomplice in a murder? It was no use trying to argue with these people. The watch, with the blood on the strap, would be the final argument. It would puzzle them, of course, but there it was. He heard in imagination the questions they would put to him.

"Why did you take the watch, if you did not murder the man?"

"Why should I have taken it if I did murder him?"

"Then why did you take the watch? Explain that, if you please."

Burton reached into his jacket pocket for a handkerchief and his hand touched the watch. He looked at his hand when he withdrew it, as though he feared it would show some sign of the contact. The guards stared at him coldly.

The murmur of voices went on behind the closed door. Burton got up from his chair and paced. He had taken only one turn when the door from the corridor was opened and there entered the plain-clothes man who had played the principal part in the comedy of the shadowers that morning.

"Mr. Burton!" He smiled amiably. "We meet again once more. I am sent for your interpreter to the Colonel Jaffke."

"In there!" Burton scowled.

When the inner door opened, he tried to catch a glimpse of Anna, but she was not in the line of vision. He walked to and fro, trying not to worry about the watch. He had to think of some way to get Anna out of it. He had begged her to leave before the police arrived, but she had been firm in her refusal.

The inner door opened again and he was told to enter. They had placed Anna in a chair close to the window and a group round her was just breaking up. She was pale and evidently weary, but he could see no trace of fear in her eyes when she looked across the room at him. Nor could he read any message for him in them. She was withdrawn, neutral, remote from the scene. At first he was troubled, then reassured. Jaffke himself had a few more questions for her, and she faced him confidently. Jaffke was cold, reserved, correct. He never raised his voice. He stood between her and the horror at the desk, but the position might have been taken accidentally. All Burton could make out was that she was being asked about her acquaintance with Sokolny. It had been, she said, limited to the office. She knew nothing of the man's private life.

Jaffke gave a languid signal that he was done, and then it was Burton's turn. They left Anna in her chair and grouped themselves round him, three men and the interpreter, but Jaffke stood aside, listening and watching, his gaze flicking over constantly to Anna.

Having a voice, Burton had full assurance again. It might be a hesitant, stammering voice, but he was able to assert himself through it, to argue, to make demands, to protest. He protested that they should permit Anna Maras to leave; it was an outrage that she should be subjected needlessly to detention in this room. He demanded to know why Sesnik was not here, since Sesnik had interested himself in Sokolny and might be able to throw some light on the murder.

Protest and demand fell into a vacuum. There was a suggestion in the air of tedium, of anticlimax, as if everything had already been settled. The questions sounded perfunctory when first put, and they certainly took no life from the efforts of the interpreter. Burton described exactly what had happened from the time he left Sokolny in the office to his return from Tolnitz with Anna and the discovery of the body.

The blankness of Jaffke and the others began to cut through his assurance. He was worried again, fearing for Anna. They would arrest her with him and charge them both with murder. Motive wouldn't worry these fools. They would hang a man first and then look for motives later, if they troubled to look at all.

"I tell you someone came to the office just before we arrived," he repeated. "There was melted snow on the floor when we came in and it hadn't started to snow until a few minutes before. It was the first thing Miss Maras noticed. She drew my attention to it."

Anna spoke after the interpreter. She spoke quickly, almost urgently, but Burton had to wait for the translation.

"The lady make answer that the little water pools might have been spilt from a glass. Or, how you say it, Sokolny . . ."

Anna took it up in English. "Sokolny may have gone downstairs for something."

"But Anna, you were the first---------"

Jaffke spoke sharply, silencing him.

The interpreter explained: "The colonel say, 'Enough.' You make answer only to questions. Then you be quiet."

"I'll be damned if I will," Burton exploded. "You tell that stuffed shirt to bring Sesnik here."

The moonfaced official would see clearly that Anna and he could not be guilty of this murder. For the rest, Burton didn't care. The police could shoot Trovic and all his gang, so long as Anna was given a chance to get away.

"Go on," Burton urged the interpreter. "Tell Jaffke what I say."

Anna intervened again. "No. There is no need to trouble Commissioner Sesnik tonight. It is all settled. It is clear to Colonel Jaffke that – "The great man cut off what was clear to him with a gesture. Burton stared at Anna but could find no hint of an explanation in her face. He turned to the interpreter.

"How is it settled?"

"Settled? I have not see this word." The man struggled more with his English, wearied by the effort. "It is most simple, this case." Distracted by a stir at the door, he lapsed into his own tongue, then translated. "Sokolny makes the suicide."

"Suicide!" The echo came from the doorway in a familiar, unmistakable voice. The bassoon had joined the concert. "Poor fellow." Sesnik waddled towards the desk. "He could not suffer the pain of his teeth any longer. It is understandable, Mr. Burton, but it is a drastic cure to blow one's brains out."

# XVI

The newcomer exchanged nods with Jaffke and the two drew apart a little to talk. Burton looked at Anna again, but her face was still expressionless. He hoped that he was as successful as she had been in concealing relief at this surprising verdict. He looked from Anna to Sesnik. He had the feeling now that the thing would not pass off so easily.

Sesnik, with a word that had a reedy impatience in it, left Jaffke and moved towards the window.

"My dear Anna," he said, "I am sorry that you have been subjected to this ordeal. I had looked forward to a happier return from Tolnitz for you. I think, as Colonel Jaffke permits it, you should now go home. My car is at your service."

He gave an instruction to one of the uniformed men and escorted the girl to the door. She said good night to Burton as she passed, but there was still no signal in her eyes. He walked to the window and looked out. It was snowing lightly now. Sesnik returned from the outer office. "You will have to excuse me, my dear friend." His voice was full of sympathy. "I must acquaint myself with the full details."

"How long is this invasion going to last?" Burton demanded.

"Not long. It is Jaffke's responsibility; he is very thorough. I do not think you will be needed any more tonight. We know where to find you."

"I have a cable to send."

"About Sokolny?" Sesnik's small eyes narrowed.

"Do you think the censor would pass anything on him?"

"The censor, of course, is in a very difficult position."

"Sure. Well, he'll have no trouble with this cable. It's the planning report. If Jaffke doesn't mind, I'll type it out and take it along with me."

The sympathetic Sesnik fixed it. Burton took the translation from Sokolny's desk and sat down at Anna's typewriter. The man who had served as interpreter watched the cable sheet as it rolled from the machine. Burton glanced at him, wondering what he was making of the newspaper abbreviations. The fellow grinned, finding them amusing.

"That's that!" Burton inked in a few corrections. "Coming along with me?"

"With you?"

"Sure. More sociable than trailing, isn't it? You can keep tabs on me better." Burton reached for his coat. "How's your friend by the way; the one you had with you this morning? Have they shot him yet?"

Taken unawares, the man laughed. Then he realised that he was getting his cues mixed and straightened his face. "I do not understand," he said stiffly.

"Think it over," Burton said. "And tell the militia I'm off to the Propaganda Ministry."

From the censor's office he went to his hotel. Sokolny's watch was no longer burning the lining of his pocket, but he wanted to be rid of it, and, after looking round his room, decided on the curtain rod. The ornamental end pieces were detachable caps. The watch and strap fitted easily into the metal tube.

He had a wash, descended to the bar, and, sick of the stuff they called whisky, turned in a vodka. There was no one in the place and he felt an unusual craving to be among people. To settle down to a book or go to bed was out of the question, and, though he had not yet eaten, food had no appeal for him. The thought of it merely reminded him that he had promised to take Anna to dinner. He was worried about her and wanted to talk to her, yet felt that now he must keep away. Whether or not the police really believed in the suicide idea, they would be wondering about the implications of Sokolny's death, and it was essential to avoid suggesting to them that there was anything collusive in his relationship with Anna. He must stick to his usual routine.

The Metropole was routine. He trudged over there, but the place was dead; it usually was until the theatres were out. The band was playing in a lifeless way and a few couples on the floor moved like zombies. Burton shook himself. The funereal mood was his alone, perhaps.

Settembrini came in. Settembrini was always talkative and sometimes amusing.

"Have you seen the programme for the gala night at the opera?" he inquired. "I hear that old Riecke wanted a spot of Wagner, but I suspect that even the Meistersinger overture would be classed as deviationist. We're going all Pan-Slav. Les Sylphides, the haunting scene from Boris, an excerpt from Eugen Onegin and some ballet from Rimsky to wind up with."

He went on talking. Burton listened absently. "Kurtz is still having trouble with her knee. I believe they're going to give that new child the honour. I wish I had seen her in Swan Lake the other night. Babette something-or-other."

Burton got up.

Settembrini asked: "What's the matter with you tonight?"

"I must go back to the office. Sorry."

Jaffke and his entourage had withdrawn, taking Sokolny with them, but Sesnik was still in the inner office. He lifted himself from the chair near the window.

"I thought you might return," he said. "I've been waiting for you."

"Why?" Burton was not amiable.

"Merely out of friendship. There are ways in which I might help you." Sesnik kicked against a book that had fallen from a small table. He was *wearing galoshes over his polished shoes;* his waddling gait seemed more clumsy.

"I don't see that I need any help," Burton retorted.

"We all need help." Sesnik bent with difficulty to pick up the book. "In your case there is the problem of finding a successor to Sokolny."

"I'll do without a successor, thanks. Miss Maras and I can manage."

"No, no! I shall see that you get an excellent man. One who will be more useful."

"To me, or to you?"

Sesnik sighed. "You are always so mistrustful, my dear fellow. I wish only to be friendly. I have always a liking for men of your country."

Burton felt himself beginning to get angry again.

"Just why do you want to plant a police spy on me?" he demanded. "Or is it Jaffke's idea?"

"Jaffke is a fool. He should carry a circus tent for that troupe of his." "You don't answer me."

"The question is unworthy of you, my friend. There is no need for so much anger."

"Listen, Sesnik! You've been pestering me ever since you called me to your office about Trovic. I've given you all the information I could find in the records."

"I believe you." His tone was sad. "You have done no wrong, but others have used you and this office, and it is a little unfortunate that Sokolny is found dead in your own room. He might have chosen a more convenient spot."

"Perhaps you think I killed him? If I had, I would certainly have chosen a more convenient spot."

"Jaffke believes he committed suicide----"

"And Jaffke is a fool!"

"Wait a moment, ray friend. Give me time to finish. All the

experts confirm the colonel. The effect is of a shot fired with the pistol in contact; the weapon shows the fingerprints of the victim; there is no evidence that anyone entered the building within the possible period of the shot except yourself and Anna Maras. The only thing that is difficult to answer is the question of motive. It is easy enough to suppose that Sokolny had guilty knowledge of Trovic and his affairs and that he was silenced because his loyalty was in doubt. It is not so easy to suppose that he silenced himself. Personally I had come to the conclusion that he knew nothing; that, if anything, he was an innocent tool."

"It can't be that your conscience is troubled?"

Sesnik was puzzled. "Professionally, I've never been able to afford a conscience," he said. "I do not understand you."

"It wouldn't be the first time an innocent man had been frightened into suicide."

"So now you are with Jaffke. You have, perhaps, abandoned your ingenious little argument of the melted snow on the floor? There is no other indication of an intruder." Sesnik walked to the door and glanced at the polished floor of the outer office. "And the small pools have dried up," he added.

"What did you expect?"

"I never expect anything. If there is a fact, I look it in the face. I examine it. I take it to pieces. I put it together in another way, if it is possible to do so."

"You're facing a fact now. Is that it?" Burton demanded.

"Yes. Perhaps you can help me. At the Metropole last night Sokolny was wearing a watch on his left wrist. Tonight it was gone."

"Perhaps you would like to search me?"

"My dear friend! What an extraordinary suggestion! I merely wished to ask if you had observed the watch on Sokolny during the day; a cheap article in a chromium case?"

"He may have broken it and taken it to be repaired. He may have forgotten to put it on when he dressed. Why is it important?"

"I don't know. Any small thing may be important. This may have no significance at all, but I would like to know what has become of that watch."

"Why don't you have his lodging searched?"

"That has already been done. The watch was not found, so I'm inclined to argue that he must have been wearing it when he left home this morning."

"Where does the argument take you?"

"Nowhere. It is most inconvenient."

"Then why bother. You say that Sokolny committed suicide."

"No, no, my dear Burton. I say nothing of the sort. I leave that to Jaffke and his troupe. Like you, I am quite convinced that Sokolny was murdered."

# XVII

Sesnik persisted in a wish to be helpful. He would see that the office was fully restored by the normal hour in the morning. Also, he meant to be protective. His dear friend Burton had suffered quite enough from political irresponsibles. Furthermore, there was Anna Maras. It was not right that a young woman like Anna should be exposed to subversive influences. Not that he had any doubts of the girl. The trouble was that certain fanatics of the opposition were always trying to involve the innocent in their schemes. Perhaps Sokolny himself had, in the beginning, been victimised in just that way. And Sesnik, because of the high regard he had always had for the late Madame Maras, would be desolated if anything happened to Anna.

Perhaps the solicitous crocodile spoke in the same voice. There was certainly something saurian about Sesnik. The gentle comical mouth was so much camouflage, hiding the grim teeth in the snapping jaws.

Burton spent a restless night. The bassoon tones broke in on his snatches of sleep and kept him tossing in wakefulness. When he rose an hour earlier than usual, it was with the thought that Sesnik had demanded a key of the office not to straighten up the place but to install microphones. By the time he had finished a light breakfast, the thought had developed. The police could have gained admission at any time through the janitor, and there might have been microphones in the office since his first visit to Sesnik, or even before.

The thermometer had risen in the night; the snow had turned to slush and the gutters were flooded. Burton asked the doorman to get him a cab. His intention had been to call for Anna and warn her of Sesnik's conviction and of his own suspicion; but by the time a cab was available he had come to believe that it would be too dangerous to approach her at her *lodging, so he drove to the office instead.*

Except for a few patches of damp there was nothing to suggest that anything unusual had happened in the night. The borrowed key lay on the scrubbed desk with a note scrawled on a sheet of copy paper:

> My compliments. I trust that this will be the end of your troubles—Paul Sesnik.

Burton searched the two rooms thoroughly, but could find no trace of a microphone or new wiring. Reason told him that his fears had been foolish, but he was no longer convinced by reason. If there were microphones they would be well hidden. He hoped now that Anna would not come to the office. He wondered for a moment if she might not have fled. She was used to the role of fugitive. She could make the frontier by easy stages. She would find some way of getting across.

It seemed simple enough in fantasy, and he was on the point of meeting her in Vienna when she walked in.

He greeted her formally and continued with an unseen microphone audience in mind. He hoped that she had got some sleep, that she had recovered from the shock, and so on.

"Before you start on the planning report," he added, "I think we'd better go over to the Ministry and pick up the seats for next week."

"I'll get them, if you wish," she answered.

"No. We'll go together. Before you take your rubbers off."

She looked so puzzled that he hurried her from the office. The street was the one place where he could be sure of privacy.

"I'm not crazy," he claimed. "Just cautious. I had a nightmare about microphones. I don't mind being watched, but I draw the line at being overheard." "For your own sake, I think you should stop being helpful." She was gloomy, performing a distasteful task. "What's going on is no concern of yours."

"It is if you're mixed up in it."

"Why? You're a stranger here; you do not know what you are doing. Your best plan is to complain about my work and tell me to leave. You will get a new girl from the university; one who will not involve you in anything."

"I don't want a new girl. Your work is more than satisfactory."

"This is no time to joke."

"I'm not joking," he protested. "I'm in this and I'm going to stay in till you get out of the country."

"I cannot get out. I must stop this fanaticism before there is any more useless bloodshed. I am afraid, terribly afraid. You know well enough that Sokolny did not kill himself. When Jaffke talked of suicide, I did my best to support the false idea, but I knew before I left that Sesnik was not deceived."

"That's what I wanted to warn you about."

"I do not need any warning. Sesnik has no charge to make against me, and he cannot take action without at least some proof. He knows that President Riecke still has an affection for my father, and he is afraid of Riecke. But this does not mean that I have to be less cautious. My protection may be very limited. There is none at all for my friends."

"Or for Trovic and his friends."

She ignored the bitterness. "Your interference may work against me," she said coldly. "The thing we have to do is follow the ordinary routine, and you keep on stepping out of the routine. I do not think there are any microphones in the office."

"But you are not sure?"

"No, I am not sure, so we will have no more discussions. You will be my employer and I will be your servant. That is all."

"You mean that I can't be of any more help to you?"

She checked in her stride to look at him. "All I mean is that you must not go on taking risks. It will be much better if you discharge me. If not, I will try for approval to take other work."

"Why won't you leave the country, as your father wishes?"

"It is not so easy. I have no desire to hang myself on the barbed wire or be killed by a mine."

"There are other ways."

"They are becoming more difficult and more expensive. For those without means, there is only the frontier."

"There's this plan that Sokolny dug up."

"I know nothing of that."

He felt she was speaking the truth, but he wanted to be sure. He watched her as he went on. "Isn't your friend Trovic interested?"

"Whatever Trovic is, he is not one of those who exploit terror to make money. He has not the money to buy aeroplanes or bribe guards. Sesnik may think he belongs to that gang, but it is not true. He has spent everything he had to help a few important people to escape."

"If I arrange for your escape, will you go?"

"No."

"Sokolny gave me the address of an agent."

"My father lives on his pension. I have only my salary. How do you think I could find fifteen hundred dollars."

"I'll take care of that."

"No. It is impossible."

"You can pay me back. I'll arrange it so that you can sell a story when you get to America. You'll be working your own passage."

"You are a very good and kind friend to me, but I cannot accept." She hesitated. "Nothing will ever make me leave my father," she said. "Nor will I desert my friends. If I have grown away from some of them, it is not their fault. I am not running away."

"You're telling me that you don't believe in them any more. For heaven's sake, Anna, don't you owe yourself something?"

"You do not see it as we do." Again she hesitated. "I owe much to others for the things we shared in the war. You must forgive me. I have to work out the problems in my own way, and it is best that you know no more than you do at this moment."

He was angry suddenly. "What kind of a fool are you? Are you going to stick your neck out just because of this romantic idiocy?"

"Here is the Propaganda Ministry," she said. "It will be absurd if we both go in to get the tickets. I will go on round the corner to Radio House. My father wishes me to send him the programme for next week."

"Come back and wait for me in the vestibule."

"It is useless to talk any more."

"I'm giving you an order."

"It is not a wise order."

He watched her go on along the street, stepping confidently as if there were no slush. She was sure of herself, but that didn't mean that she knew what was round the corner. He looked up at the soaring radio mast on the tall building.

He greeted his friend in the Press Department sourly.

"Why didn't you send the tickets with the rest of the junk?" Burton demanded. "Do you think I've nothing better to do than chase round here every few minutes?"

"I'm sorry, Mr. Burton," Gregor answered him. "We always like to offer a choice of places to the foreign press on these occasions."

There was no way out. He had to go through the formalities of approving his seats. Gregor had taken special care to reserve him a good place in the reviewing stand for the big parade. He would be quite close to President Riecke himself and within hand's reach of a dozen celebrities.

"Good," Burton said disagreeably. "Where can I buy a bomb?"

Gregor smiled nervously and looked over his shoulder. "I always like your American humour," he said, managing to convey a mild reproach by slightly stressing the first person singular. "Now, there are three seats for the great presidential address at the National Theatre on Wednesday, one on the platform for yourself, and two at the press table for Miss Maras and Mr. Sokolny."

"Mr. Sokolny will not be using his."

"I'm sorry. Is it his teeth?"

So they were hushing it up completely. A trip to the mortuary and no one would hear any more of the remains. Burton wondered if there was any next of kin.

"I want seats for the Opera Gala on Tuesday," he said. "I'll take the agency coverage on most of the smaller things."

"But you will attend the Ranawitz ceremony on the Saturday?"

"Ranawitz?"

Burton remembered with an effort. The Guernica, the Lidice of local tradition. Some peasant had dared to fire a shot in defence of his home, and a village had been wiped out. The invader had ordered total destruction, but had carelessly left a few stones to stand as a monument of his ruthlessness. Each year, after the rejoicings in the capital, there was a pilgrimage to the common burial place of the martyrs. The relatives of the dead were honoured on this day of remembrance. There were solemn affirmations. There was much political psalm singing.

"No," Burton said. "I shall not be going to Ranawitz." "I'm sorry to hear that." Gregor raised a tone of mild protest. "Your predecessor, Mr. Glover, always made a point of going to Ranawitz. It is a very pleasant trip and we provide an excellent train for officials and the press."

"You'll be able to fill the train without me. Send the other tickets along to me when you will."

"Tomorrow," Gregor promised. "President Riecke is arriving from the country on Sunday. There will be a press conference at the Imperi ... - At the official residence at five o'clock.

Here is your pass. It is not transferable. Any questions you wish to put must reach this office not later than noon tomorrow."

"That means I'll get no sleep tonight."

Gregor smiled nervously again. "Sign for the pass, please," he requested.

Anna was not in the vestibule. Burton walked back to the office in a bad temper. She was there at her desk, a picture of calm efficiency.

"I thought I said----" He began coldly, and then stopped as he became aware of a flaxen-haired youth rising from a chair in Sokolny's corner.

"Who's this?" he demanded.

Anna answered the question. "His name is Wenzl. He has come to take Sokolny's place."

"Oh, has he!" Burton advanced grimly on the youth. "If you're not out of this office in ten seconds, Mr. Wenzl, you'll go out on the seat of your pants. You can go back to Sesnik and tell him that when I want a man, I pick him myself."

"I am from the university, sir," Wenzl protested timidly. "Mr. Sesnik was so kind to recommend----"

"You've got two seconds left."

Wenzl fled.

"You shouldn't have done that," Anna said. "The boy may have worked out all right. Sesnik will be offended."

Burton strode into his room and slammed the door.

# XVIII

There was no move from Sesnik. It could scarcely be sulks or indifference, so Burton decided that the policeman must be too concerned with polishing up his shoes for the week ahead to bother about anything else. There was an appearance of peace in the office. Work dropped into a dull routine. Anna dug into the accumulation of newspapers on her desk and after a while uncovered the waiting box of chocolates. Burton was at the water filter.

"Thank you," she said. "You are very kind."

He looked across at her. "Sorry. I forgot to tell you. A gift from Sesnik, while you were away."

She coloured a little. Then she shrugged, replaced the lid, and dropped the box into the wastebasket.

"Mr. Sesnik is grotesque." Her eyes had a hardness that he had not seen in them before. "Next time he will come, perhaps, with pieces of silver. That will, at least, be less insulting."

The suggestion behind her words worried Burton. Sesnik had been cheated of one informer. If he really believed that Anna could help him, he would act soon and ruthlessly. He might wait till Riecke had paid his visit to the capital, but he would wait no longer. Meanwhile, Anna would be kept under surveillance.

Like Sokolny!

The thought made him shiver. If Anna were not to be lost in the whirlpool of intrigue which was already drawing her towards its centre, he would have to plunge into it himself.

On Saturday the snow and the slush were gone and in bright sunshine the town broke out bunting, hoisted flags, and erected gigantic pictures of Riecke and other heroes of the new order. From his office window, Burton could see as far as the Alexis Bridge. There were tall poles on the bridge with looped streamers of red bunting. Beyond was the great square, where the workmen were busy on the saluting base and the stands for the privileged spectators.

Burton hauled on his overcoat and took up his hat.

"I'll be out for a while," he told Anna.

He went to his room in the hotel to recover Sokolny's watch, then walked to the shop of Emil Dovinye, four doors from the Alexis Bridge.

A tall man with a pointed grey beard came from behind a partition. It was quiet in the shop except for the ticking of clocks. Burton remembered that the watchmaker spoke French.

He said, "Are you Monsieur Dovinye? I have a watch to be repaired. Examine it, please."

Dovinye turned the winder, opened the case, and fixed the lens of his craft in his eye.

"There is nothing wrong with this watch," he said.

"Nevertheless, it needs your attention. You have been strongly recommended to me. I believe you have seen the watch before."

"It has been here for repair. Where did you get it?"

"From a man named Sokolny. My name is Burton. Possibly you have heard of me. Is there a place where we may talk?"

"This is as good as any. Customers may be seen before they enter."

In the street, a man in a shabby coat was peering at the few articles in the window.

Burton removed his own wrist watch. "I think you had better sell me a new strap. You have a card in the window."

Dovinye came from behind the counter and took up the card of straps from the window. The man in the shabby coat sauntered along the quay. Burton said, "There has been some trouble. Sokolny is dead."

"Dead?" It was news to Dovinye. He was alarmed.

Burton reassured him and supplied a few details. He said, "It is necessary for a friend if mine to take a trip abroad. I am willing to pay well if it can be arranged. I understand a tour is being organised."

"I don't know about such things."

"Perhaps you can send me to someone who does?"

Dovinye hesitated. "It is difficult. You are a stranger to me."

"But you have the watch."

"I will consult and let you know. There is a further difficulty because Sokolny is dead. If you will wait a moment. . . ."

The moment stretched into minutes. Dovinye was using a telephone, or he had slipped out the back way to see somebody. Burton looked through the window along the quay, but the man in the shabby coat was not in sight.

Dovinye came back. "I am required to make sure that you are Monsieur Burton of the American newspaper."

"That's easy enough." Burton produced his identity card with photograph and signature. "Do you want me to sign my name for you?"

"If you please."

Dovinye compared the signatures and nodded. He said, "I suggest that you see Carlo Settembrini, the photographer."

Burton made a noise that was something like a whistle.

"You are surprised," Dovinye commented.

"A little. You'd better keep Sokolny's watch. How much do I owe you for the strap?"

"One hundred dollars American. It is the best pigskin. Killing pigs is a very risky business."

# XIX

Burton thought he knew Settembrini well enough to go straight to the point. "I've just come from Dovinye," he announced.

"Dovinye?" Settembrini repeated. "Do I know anyone of that name?"

"Yes. The watchmaker on the Breclin Quay. I'm acting for a friend."

"A case of claustrophobia?"

"If you want to call it that. I understand the treatment costs fifteen hundred dollars. I'm ready to pay."

"The cost is slightly more at present. The equipment used is very expensive."

"And the risks have to be paid for. I know."

Settembrini's eyes narrowed slightly. "That is not very polite, my dear Burton."

"Don't be so sensitive. You must admit that, for me, this is all a bit surprising."

"I don't pretend to be a philanthropist, but there is something more than money in this. When you are over your surprise, tell me about the patient."

"The name is Anna Maras. The other day you wondered what had become of her. She works for me."

"So that is why you came to pump me!" Settembrini laughed. "I am beginning to scent more than a journalistic interest."

"Scent what you like. Her father wants to get her out of the country."

"I can understand that. He must feel quite unsafe with such a hostage to consider. Does she consent to go?"

"Not yet. I'm hoping to persuade her." "It may not be necessary if it is just a matter of getting her across the frontier. Once out, she would not be likely to come back, would she?"

Burton stared. "Are you suggesting that she could be abducted?"

"Taken unawares would be a better description. Since she is on your staff it might be worked, if things go according to plan."

"What is the plan?"

"I'm not going to answer any questions about that. I can tell you only that the organisation is elaborate."

"How soon will it be put into effect?"

"On the day of the memorial ceremony at Ranawitz. We are taking advantage of the traffic to the village, which is very close to the frontier. If you can arrange for the girl to be on a certain train, we will be able to take care of her. Our difficulty is to get official travel permits. That will be easy for you."

"Which train is she to travel by?"

"It will not be decided until next week. Three trains leave in the morning of the big day. One of them will be selected for our party."

"How many will be in the party?"

Settembrini frowned. "There will be no more questions, please. The cost to you will be seventeen hundred dollars. You will see that a thousand is paid to my agent in Rome. You may hand the remaining seven hundred to me. Any extra travel permits you may be able to get, I will buy from you at a hundred dollars each."

"It's a nice offer, but I'm not opening a business."

"Your scruples do you honour, my dear Burton. Be grateful that we do not share them. If you decide to sponsor your young friend's journey, you will let me know positively by Tuesday night. You will be going to the Opera Gala? I will see you there. We will have the train fixed by then." "Is it going to be very dangerous?"

"Not if things go as planned." Settembrini smiled confidently. "We are reducing risk to a minimum. It is always my aim to make everything foolproof. Up to date our casualty figures compare favourably with those of the normal transport facilities. We are proud of that."

"You ought to advertise."

Settembrini smiled. "The only thing that makes me uneasy," he said, "is the general atmosphere. If I were a meteorologist, I would be inclined to forecast some kind of storm. I feel there is something working up. Something . . . Maybe it is just the big week ahead, the tension on the eve of festivities. Do you sense anything?"

"I haven't thought. The last few days have been busy."

Burton hesitated, came to a decision, and gave the news of Sokolny's end. This was Settembrini's cue to whistle. He still had his lips pursed when Burton went on.

"Sokolny was one of your agents, wasn't he?"

Settembrini shook his head absently. He was busy with his own thoughts.

"One thing is certain," Burton said: "Sokolny was murdered to stop his mouth. He had been seen in Sesnik's company at the Metropole."

"There are so many factions, and most of them are charged with fanaticism," Settembrini said slowly. "We, on the other hand, are hard realists. As a realist, I am worried, Burton. Sokolny was not killed because he was one of our agents. We are too well organised for that. This thing is deeper, and I think you know it. You are frightened for the girl. I am frightened, too, for our beautiful plan. We have invested a lot of money in it, and it could be wrecked so easily by these psychotics who think they are patriots. I tell you, Burton, there is something in the air. I have felt it for days. Earthquake weather." Burton said, "Shall I take the address of your Rome agent?"

Settembrini shook his head. "I am not the final voice. There may be objections to Miss Maras. I will speak to you at the opera in the first intermission. Meanwhile you should arrange for the girl to go to the ceremony at Ranawitz."

Burton was impatient now, and the appointed day seemed too far away. While he waited for Gregor at the Propaganda Ministry he studied the programme for the all-important week:

| | | |
|---|---|---|
| **Sunday:** | **Arrival of President Riecke** | 12 noon. |
| | **Press Conference** | 5 pm |
| | **Radio Broadcast** | 9 pm |
| **Monday:** | **Grand Commemorative Parade** | 10 am |
| **Tuesday:** | **Gala Performance at Opera** | 8 pm |
| **Wednesday:** | **President's Annual Address at National Theatre** | 3 pm |
| **Thursday:** | **Inspection of Factories** | |
| **Friday:** | **Schools and Hospitals** | |
| **Saturday:** | **Anniversary Ceremony at Ranawitz** | 12 noon. |

Gregor came along to attend to him.

"I've changed my mind about Ranawitz," Burton said. "I'll need two tickets, one for Miss Maras."

"It is just as well that I held them for you," Gregor growled amiably. "I thought you would come to realise the national significance of the occasion."

"I have," Burton agreed. "I was entirely wrong."

Gregor made out the tickets and permits. "Unfortunately, I can no longer grant you de luxe seats on the special train," he said. "You will have to take your chance with other passengers on one of the earlier trains."

Burton told Anna as soon as he got back to the office. "We're going to cover the Ranawitz show after all. Both of us." She made no comment. She said, "Sesnik telephoned to know how you were."

"What did he want?"

"Just that. I told him you were very well."

"Remind me next week to ask after his health. We mustn't neglect these courtesies."

She smiled, but the gloom that had been upon her since Sokolny's death quickly descended again. Burton saw that she felt herself bound by her loyalties to an inevitable fate and would make no attempt to free herself.

He would have to make the attempt for her.

# XX

The President arrived at noon on Sunday to a ringing of bells and a sounding of whistles. Burton had his first sight of the great man when he attended the press conference at the official residence, formerly the Imperial Palace. Riecke looked very old and very tired, and his lined grey face suggested an unwrapped mummy rather than a living man. He was tall and very thin and stoop-shouldered, and his dull dark eyes peered through thick-lensed spectacles. When he acknowledged the welcoming cheers of the assembly with a bow, his head seemed insecurely fixed upon him. The semi-military tunic he wore was ill-fitting, as if his frame had shrunk since he had put it on. Halvic, the chief aide, a hustling, self-important man, stood on one side of him; on the other was Varlein, the dynamic secretary of the Party.

Riecke, after his bow, stood like a somnambulist while Halvic made a few introductory remarks. The proceedings were infinitely boring. Riecke delivered a brief speech composed entirely of platitudes. Then the selected questions were put to him and he repeated the same platitudes with little variation. When he hesitated, Halvic prompted him. When he was finished with each question, he sat down and appeared to concentrate on the French and German echoing from the interpreters.

Not a line of copy was to be extracted from the thin-voiced patter. Burton gave up following the words and studied the enigma from which they came. Settembrini's satirical summing up came back to him. Here was the beautifully constructed puppet in action. But at some time or other the man must have had some inner force to drive him beyond the confines of a university. No leader himself, perhaps, his career had at least been distinguished enough to qualify him for nominal leadership. 'Gentle, benevolent, fond of children . . .' More than that to it, but there was little trace of anything now. The man was a sad figure, and it was not merely with the sadness of approaching senility. It was in his loneliness, perhaps. Or had there crept into the dream the thought that things were not all they seemed, or should be?

In the evening the thin, aged voice went out over the air from Radio House and loud-speakers on street corners conveyed the empty message to those who had no sets of their own to switch on. Burton stood with Anna on the steps of St. Trophimus and watched the knot of people round one of the amplifiers. They were silent people. They seemed unmoved. They had heard it all before. It was traditional, like the militiamen in their greatcoats on the fringes of the little throng.

"All we need is some music by Moussorgsky," Burton remarked. "And a few knouts."

"I do not understand," the girl said stiffly.

"You're always quoting Boris at me. Can't I be permitted an allusion? Riecke would make a good tsar, especially with Varlein and Halvic to prompt him. An innocent despot. No hauntings, no striking clocks."

"What do you know about Riecke?" "Enough for myself. I'd like to know what these people think of him."

"They will wait all night in the cold to see him."

"Or to see the circus. Let's take a look at the square."

The Great Square was full of people and all the unreserved space in front of the reviewing stand was already taken up. The militia had defined the wide lane for the parade and they were there in strength to keep the crowds in order. Beyond a sweep of lawn, the Renaissance façade of the official residence was floodlit, but there was nothing to show that it housed the captive Riecke. Braziers burned in the square to give warmth to the guards. The people had only their coats and the rugs they had brought. Sometimes a group started a song, but it rarely found many supporters. Perhaps the night was too cold. Following the President's broadcast the amplifiers were silent, but at ten they would be linked again to Radio House and there would be music.

Burton saw Anna's strained, tired face. He took her arm to guide her through the press that was filling in round them, and realised that she was trembling.

She said, "If you can manage without me, I would like to go home.

"But we were going to dinner," he protested. "It's been outstanding since Tolnitz. I've only a few lines to dictate. Then we'll go to the Metropole."

"I'm sorry. I don't think I could eat anything."

"Are you sick?" He took her by the arm again, but she now had herself under control.

She shook her head. "I am tired."

"Okay, I'll walk with you to the bus. Have you got your seat for the parade tomorrow with you, or did you leave it at the office?"

She opened her handbag, took out the card, and offered it to him. "I would rather not use it," she said. "You could give it to one of your friends."

"Look here, what is this?" he said harshly.

"I can be of no help to you." She looked back at the square apprehensively. "I'd rather not be there. I don't want to see **it.**"

"Are you working for me, or aren't you? I just want to know." He pushed the card back into the bag angrily. "You've a job to do tomorrow. You're to cover the women's contingents. Is that clear?"

"Very well."

She shut the bag. She did not speak again until she said good night at the bus stop. That was all she said.

Back at the office, he rolled a sheet into the typewriter and smacked out "Add Riecke" as if he wanted the letters to bite through the paper. He leaned back in the chair and looked across the machine at the wall in front of him. He was trying to think what he wanted to add to the Riecke story, but all he could think of was Anna. Instead of the opera bill on the wall he saw the dedicated, Antigone-like face of the girl. She was changed; there was nothing of the former Anna left. And the lost Anna had become more desirable. He had to face it. He had never wanted anything so much as he now wanted Anna Maras.

He typed a few lines, then wrenched the paper from the machine and hurled it in a crumpled ball across the room. There was another image before him then. Pero Trovic.

# XXI

The stoop-shouldered professor wore army uniform, and the medals pinned across his tunic seemed to drag him down. He began to button his greatcoat over his chest the moment he stepped from his car, and Halvic, like a good valet, came to his assistance. A great cheer rang out over the square, and massed bands played noisily. All the spectators in the stands rose up and the wooden structures swayed crazily. There was a pause. Riecke stood with his white head bared to the sun. Then he moved slowly down the line of the guard of honour, turned, came back, and mounted the six steps of the red-carpeted platform, where the city and service functionaries waited to greet him. He stared forward at the front row of spectators at the rear of the wide platform, and Burton had the uncomfortable feeling that the aged eyes were focussing on him. The old man peered through his thick-lensed glasses. A few minutes later, when he was seated, he turned and peered again, moving his chair to get clear of an obstructing figure.

The show began at once and went on for hour after hour through the morning. Planes flew past, tanks and guns rumbled across the square, men marched, women marched, children marched. It was like every show of its kind, and Burton had tired of it before it began. All he was conscious of was Anna sitting impassively at his side.

There came a break in the parade, and once more the eyes of President Riecke were turned in his direction, but this time Burton became aware that it was Anna who was the object of the President's attention. When, at some time past noon, the last section of the procession had marched across the square, the old man thrust aside the restraining hand of Halvic and pushed through his entourage towards the girl.

Burton saw that she was embarrassed. She knew that the great man was doing the wrong thing. He was rarely permitted to step from his part in private; to do so in public was an enormity. But he was old and scarcely conscious of the myth he had become, and he would have his way.

"It is Anna," he said in his thin voice.

"Yes," she answered, and she smiled at him, calling him "dear Uncle." He took her hands and held them while he talked to her, and Burton made out that he was asking about her father and regretting that he had not seen him for so long a time.

Varlein tried to intervene. The programme. The car was waiting. The timetable was most important.

Riecke turned on him angrily. Varlein stepped back at a snarled command, and, like Halvic, was nonplussed. They could not reveal by as much as a shrug what they thought of the old fool. They knew him only too well in these moods. Next thing he'd be taking the Maras girl along in the car with him and sitting her next to him at table. But the Maras girl had sense enough to see that the situation was precarious.

"You must go, dear Uncle," she said. "All the people are waiting for you."

"Yes," he answered. "They are always waiting for me. When I am home again you must come to me and bring Anton. We will talk."

He stumbled a little as he moved towards the steps, but Varlein and Halvic were there, one on either side of him. In a few seconds the car conveyed him to the portico of the official residence, a distance of two hundred yards or so, and the crowd, breaking up, swarmed across the square.

There was little to be written about the parade that had not been written a hundred times before. Burton did not return to the office until after lunch, and by that time Anna had completed her section.

"I have done what you wished," she said. "Will you really send such nonsense?"

"Maybe."

"I would like to leave early. I want to go out to Tolnitz."

"You may leave now, if you wish."

"Thank you." She hesitated. "Have you thought over what I said about discharging me?" "You still want to be released?" he inquired.

"Yes."

"Okay. We'll make it a week's notice. Your last job will be the Ranawitz ceremony. Will that suit you?"

She seemed a little shocked, as if she had not expected so prompt a surrender.

"Yes," she said. "It will suit."

He had it planned now. He would commit her completely to Settembrini's party. He would see Anton Maras and get him to write a letter to be delivered to her when she was across the frontier. He would make sure that Maras urged her not to return, and he would himself write another letter, which she would take to Bob Kinder Mann in Vienna. Perhaps he would never see her again, but that would be up to her.

"Meanwhile," he said, "there's the Opera Gala tomorrow night. I shall want you to come with me."

He was using his position unfairly, and in the moment of speaking he saw that it was a useless thing to do. He was making a fool of himself in her eyes. He decided to change the implied order into an invitation.

"That is, if you'd care to," he added.

"I'll be very glad to come."

Her voice had warmth again, and next day there was a return to the old friendliness. He might have reflected bitterly that this was all in gratitude for her supposed release at the end of the week, but he wanted to think that there was a little more than this to it. He called for her in a cab, and when they joined the excited throng in the brilliantly lit Opera House, he thought she had never looked more lovely.

"If your dear uncle sees you tonight," he said, "he'll invite you to the State Box."

"Poor old man." She smiled. "I think he is very lonely these days."

The box was empty, yet eyes were constantly turning towards it, noting the details, the emblems, the flags, the greenery of pot plants. Burton wondered if the attendant he had encountered on his last visit to the opera would be there to open the door for the official party. It would be in the man's charge— the fifth box from the proscenium on the Grand Tier.

The chatter tonight seemed to rise in pitch with the intensity of expectation. People looked at watches, and looked again a minute later. There was more excitement in the tuning up noises of the orchestra. The conductor came to his desk amid applause, but the house lights were not lowered, and the conductor waited, like all the rest. He stood there relaxed for a moment, then suddenly tightened up, rapped on his desk, and lifted his baton. The orchestra was on its feet, the whole house rose, a discreet spotlight picked out the box, and the old man stepped forward, followed by Varlein, Halvic, and the chiefs of the Army and Air Force in uniform.

Everyone stood rigid while the orchestra played the "Internationale." It was impressive. The house was devout. Then, at the close, the cheers and hand clapping swelled up and the old man bowed and bowed again. Against the background of uniforms he was a simple figure in a dark tunic with a military collar. He wore only one decoration, the medal of honour given him by his own Supreme Council.

The house lights faded, a hush followed the noise, once more the conductor rapped on his desk, and quickly, almost before the audience could settle down, the performance of Les Sylphides began.

Babette danced. Up to the last minute Vera Kurtz had had treatments, but had been compelled to remain in her dressing room. Once more Babettte started shakily, but gained control of herself before the end. Anna complained when the lights came up. "She will not relax. She worries too much."

"Yes. You wait here." Burton looked at the crush in the aisles. "I said I'd see Settembrini about some pictures." Settembrini was waiting in the bar. He said, "We are ready to take the girl. Have you decided?"

Burton nodded. "She has not yet consented, so you'll have to make the necessary arrangements."

Settembrini smiled and made a magician's pass with his hands. "All the arrangements have been completed. There is only one thing for you to do. Put her on the nine-o'clock train from the Alexis Station."

"There'll be letters to give her when she's clear."

"Let me have them before Friday. And be careful, Burton, how you behave. If you rouse any suspicion, the Police Judiciary will make it impossible for you to continue your work here. They are used to putting two and two together. They have even been known to do more complicated sums. There is a man standing at the end of the bar at this moment—the one with the glass of tea in his hand. Do you see him? He is quite a mathematician. He has been eyeing us ever since we pushed out of the crowd into this quiet corner. By the way, the watchmaker Dovinye was arrested this morning. Please keep your face straight."

"Sesnik?"

"I believe so."

"Because of my visit?"

"The whole world goes to a watchmaker. It is a question whether Sokolny was liquidated soon enough."

"Then you may be in danger?"

"I don't think so. Dovinye had other irons in the fire. There is nothing to show that he sent you to me. We are, after all, old acquaintances."

"But they have ways. He may talk."

"No, my friend, Dovinye will not talk. He always carried with him some cyanide. He had the good sense to swallow it." Settembrini laughed. "You had better rejoin the beautiful Anna. The first bell has gone. Starensky is in good voice just now and you mustn't miss him. It is true he is no Chaliapin, but he has the advantage of still being alive. It is a pity they are not doing the end of Boris instead of the second act. I suppose they have to concede something to the revered Riecke. He thinks Rimsky's orchestration of the haunting scene the best music since the Devil's Glen."

The sarcasm was wasted on Burton. He fingered the new strap of his wrist watch as if it were fastened too tightly for his comfort.

Anna was not in her seat. He looked round the crowded house uneasily. People were hurrying along the aisles and settling themselves. President Riecke and his party were conversing at the back of their box. Riecke moved forward to his chair and the others followed his example with the self-conscious ease of the great.

As Burton looked round once more, he caught sight of Anna in the Grand Tier box from which he had seen the opening of Prince Igor. She was talking to a young man; then, a moment later, she was leaving him, and she regained her seat just as the lights were dimmed down.

"I saw a friend of mine," she said.

The orchestra had begun and a moment later the curtain rose on an apartment in the Kremlin. Burton looked up at the box from which Anna had come. The young man was leaning forward from one of the rear seats and his face was clearly visible in the light from the stage. Burton was sure he had never seen him before. He looked again, then turned to glance at Anna. Her eyes were fixed on the scene. She seemed serene, relaxed. He watched her, and saw her lean forward slightly. Boris had entered, and Starensky really was in good voice.

The whole house was tense as the scene developed. The lighter moments with the children were over. Boris meditated sadly the unrest in his kingdom. Shuisky came to tell of rebellion in Poland. Dmitri was on the march, the false Dmitri, for the true tsarevitch had been slain; Shuisky himself could bear witness to the crime, and did so, leaving Boris in the grip of his torturing conscience. Now the score spun to the climax of the striking-clock scene. Haunted by the vision of the murdered Dmitri, Boris shrank in terror. The great moment for the rapt spectators had come. Boris tottered and fell upon his knees, and at that instant a woman screamed wildly in the auditorium.

Like others who were startled by the scream, Burton looked up at the Grand Tier. His eyes went to the box that Anna had visited. The first thing he saw was light from the corridor through the open door of the box. Two figures moved against the square of light. One was the young man Anna had spoken to, the other was Trovic.

He had pushed the screaming woman roughly aside. Now he leapt on to the balustrade and flung something violently into the State Box. Helvic threw himself in front of Riecke in hopeless effort to deflect the missile. There was a flash of light and a shattering detonation and dust blotted out the flag-hung box. Then stuttering through the screams of terror, came the sound of a machine pistol.

Burton discovered that he was holding Anna protectively, his arms round her, pressing her close to him. He must have wheeled and grasped her the moment he saw Trovic's arm go up for the throw. He turned again to peer at the State Box through the cloud of plaster dust.

President Riecke hung limply over the wreckage of the balustrade, among the shredded flags. Where his face had been there was now no more than a pulp of blood.

Then the panic began.

# XXII

Burton was forced into the aisle by the rush towards the exits, but managed to keep his hold on Anna. For a moment they were borne along, helpless against the pressure; then he pushed the girl between two rows of deserted seats and waited with her. Others, scattered in twos and threes over the floor of the house, had similarly found refuge from the mad crush of screaming women and yelling men.

The great golden curtain was down, but Burton had no recollection of its being lowered. He had had a vague glimpse of people running across the stage, of an astonished Boris peering out across the footlights. Other impressions remained more vivid in his mind. Trovic had turned and raced from the box, following the young man who had helped him. Perhaps they had escaped through the pass door and out onto the steps at the side of the Opera House. Perhaps they had failed to reach the pass door. There had been a lot of shooting after the bomb explosion. Now something was happening outside, in the square or beyond. More shooting.

Suddenly the panic was over. Frantic people still pressed towards the exits, but there was no more struggling. Uniformed police were everywhere, shouting orders to control what was left of the crowd. There were casualties on the floor; people had been crushed, knocked down, trampled on. And more casualties from the bomb. One partition of the State Box had been blown out and occupants of the next box had been killed or injured. Ambulance men were busy with stretchers.

"We've got to get out of here," Burton said.

Anna seemed too shaken even to know what he was saying. She put a hand to her head as if she were trying to capture some elusive thought. A sob shook her. "Oh my God," she said.

He took her arm. "Come on, Anna. Let's go."

"Yes." She clung to his arm.

Crowds swarmed on the portico and down the steps and there were more police with more orders. The shooting was still going on, somewhere near the river. Burton hurried Anna through the press of people and out into the square.

"You were in that box at the interval," Burton said. "Did you know that your friend was helping Trovic?"

In the bright lights from the great façade of the opera he could see her look of blank surprise. It changed to one of alarm.

"I must go to Babette," she said.

Probably she needed Babette more than Babette needed her. He did not know. He had to get her to some place of safety so that he would be free to find out what was happening.

"You haven't answered my question," he said.

"It is too foolish to answer."

He walked with her towards the stage door.

There had been silence for a moment or two, but now came a more vehement burst of firing from the direction of the river. She clung to his arm, pressing tightly with her fingers. When he turned his head to look at her, he saw that tears were at last streaming down her cheeks.

"You should go straight home," he said.

"No. I must see Babette. If you are going to the office, I will follow you later."

That was better. She was taking hold of herself again. "If I'm not there, wait for me," he told her. "I must get the news."

He was thinking that he should have gone at once to the Grand Tier, but he had been too worried about the girl. Now, pushing through the crowd to the portico again, he encountered Mervan and

Attridge. "They won't let you get near anyone," Attridge warned him. "What's the use, anyway? The censor will clamp down on everything except the official handout."

"What have you got hold of?" Burton asked.

"Riecke was killed instantly. Varlein's still alive, but damaged. I don't know how seriously. Halvic and the service chiefs escaped with minor injuries."

"The next box was a shambles." Mervan took up the story. "All killed. Two officials and their wives."

"And a dozen or so minor casualties round about," Attridge added. "Get my name right if you mention it." He laughed, showing a bleeding wrist. "I guess the bodyguards will be digging their own graves by dawn."

"What happened to the assassin?" Burton held Attridge by the sleeve.

"There were two of them. They both got clean away. Nice neat plan, if you ask me. They just vanished."

Of course. The pass door, the stairway, the exit on the side of the house. Trovic knew all the ins-and-outs of the building, just as Babette did. The pass door was very convenient, but it had to be opened from the stage side.

Babette?

He pushed the thought away as Settembrini jostled towards them, equipped with camera and flash bulbs.

"What's the news from Radio House?" he asked.

"What should be the news?" Mervan demanded. "Is that where all the shooting was?"

"Is," Settembrini corrected. "Listen to it. I don't know the truth of it, but they say Radio House has been taken."

"Taken?" Burton echoed. "What do you mean, taken?"

"The assassination was the signal for a rising, a coup." Settembrini was enjoying it to the full. "Here, wait a minute; Tuvanye may know something."

Tuvanye was a portly citizen with the sweat of haste on his

brow. He had been running and was a little breathless. "The Army has revolted," Settembrini translated. "The general staff has been seized and executed. The troops are marching on the capital with guns and tanks. Not only Radio House, but the transmitter station and the Post and Telegraph Building have been captured. I wonder."

But they were in too much of a hurry to care what he wondered.

"Let's go!" Attridge interrupted him. Mervan was already dancing down the steps in a state of high excitement. This was what he had been waiting for.

Settembrini fell in beside Burton.

"I am afraid," he said. "Things do not work out so easily."

Things had worked out easily enough at the Opera House. To time. Perhaps to a bar of music. The clock had been striking for Tsar Boris. But Burton was now the haunted one, with the face of the dazed Anna before him as he strode on with Settembrini.

There was no more shooting. Everything seemed to have fallen into a dead calm ahead of them. Traffic had ceased, pedestrians padded quietly as if they were on some clandestine mission. Then suddenly the calm was broken by the cry of a dozen trumpets. A fanfare blared out from all the loud-speakers on the street comers, and Burton halted to listen.

"This is it," Settembrini remarked. "Authentic. Straight from the horse's mouth."

The voice came over the air, using simple words in simple phrases. Burton could understand most of it; Settembrini translated the rest.

"I speak to my countrymen," the voice said. "I speak to the humble peasant and to the highest in the land. I have news for you. Tonight a tyrant has gone the way of all tyrants. The hated Riecke, who stood with the oppressors of the people, has been executed by the forces of the true freedom. Those forces are now in control. We call to you who love your land to join with us in stamping out an order that has brought suffering upon you. We bring you liberty. We are in control of "

The voice was cut off abruptly.

"They are not in control of the switches, anyway," Settembrini commented. "I've got to get busy."

Burton paid no attention. He could think only that the voice was the voice of Pero Trovic, the assassin.

Settembrini waved as he hurried away.

A great crowd had collected in the roadway near Radio House; inoffensive onlookers, curious to know what was going on. They stood motionless till a troop of mounted police arrived and began to force them back. Then they broke and swayed and pushed and shouted. Burton saw one of the horses rear up. A woman screamed. Men leapt at the trooper and tore him from his horse. Then the long sticks were out as the police rode into the mob. More screams. Someone fired a pistol. Missiles flew through the air, and in the next few minutes one might have gained the impression that the people were responding to the radio appeal.

Burton was caught in an eddying movement of the mass and carried back to the end of the street. The wild tumult died. The police were a line of equestrian statues across the roadway, beyond them a dozen or more casualties lay groaning on the cobbles.

Suddenly the voice of Trovic again blared out from the loudspeakers, beginning in midsentence.

". . . suffering upon you. We bring you liberty. We are in control of the radio system and will broadcast news from moment to moment. The Army marches with us to strike off your chains. Rise, rise, rise! The new dawn is yours."

A band played a popular march of the Resistance, and then the voice began again. "I speak to my countrymen. I speak to the humble peasant and to the highest in the land . . ."Over and over, and nothing else happened.

Burton moved on hurriedly. Attridge had beaten him to the Post and Telegraph Building, but it seemed that the news of its capture had been premature. Attridge had tried to slip a cable through and had been referred to the Foreign Press Censorship.

"I'm on my way to see what has happened over there."

Burton joined him. The familiar office was crowded with correspondents. Someone had turned on a radio and the recorded voice of Trovic was still repeating its call to the people.

A typewritten sheet on the notice board conveyed the information in German, French, and English that no messages for transmission abroad would be accepted till further notice. There was the further information that all departments of the Propaganda Ministry were closed for the night.

# XXIII

Burton started for the office. Crowds moved without purpose in the streets, or stood in groups, talking excitedly, listening to the tireless voice that filled the air with its parrot exhortations. At last another voice intervened, giving news of the casualties at the opera, but there was nothing that Burton had not already learned.

When he reached the office building, the janitor was missing. He ran up the stairs, hoping to find Anna. She was not there, and suddenly his anxiety became an agony of misgiving. With the whole town in a ferment, anything might have happened to her on the way.

He saw again the horses ridden into the surging crush of people. She might have been one of the victims left lying in the roadway. Certainly he should have insisted on her going straight home from the Opera House, with or without Babette.

He went to the window and looked out. The lighted tower of Radio House rose behind the dark dome of St. Trophimus. From the street below the voice of Trovic reached him, muted but articulate. Once more it was cut off in mid-sentence as if the needle had been lifted from the record, but something more drastic had happened. The lights in the tower had gone out.

Burton paced, but always he returned to the window. Once he raised the bottom sash and listened. There was silence. The whole town seemed dead, yet the lamps burned brightly in the streets, and the way down to the Alexis Bridge was almost as clear as by day. The frosty air bit into the room; Burton closed the window and switched on an electric fire.

He thought again about Anna. Even if he were unable to get a cab, he could walk to Anna's lodging. If she hadn't reached home, he would try the Treplevs' flat. Babette would know.

A sound from the outer office made him pause. The door was opened and Anna and Babette were there, looking like two distraught ghosts. Burton went to them with a sigh of relief. Babette seemed near exhaustion, shivering, holding on Anna's arm for support. There were still traces of stage makeup on her face and the marks of tears were plain. All her prettiness was gone; two hours had made her old.

Anna said, "I could not leave her. She wanted to come, to see if there was any news. We are very cold."

"There's heat in my room." He took Babette into his office. Looking after her friend had helped Anna recover. She went briskly to her desk for a match and started a flame under the tea urn. She had, he thought, turned to the rigid self-discipline of the Resistance days. As long as there was something to do, fear and exhaustion could be ignored. "The police held us at the Opera House," she said. "Sesnik was there."

"Did he ask you about your visit to that box?"

"No. I think you are the only one who saw me."

"Who was that young man?"

"A friend. I told you."

"What is his name?"

"What name he is using now I do not know. His real name does not matter."

"What does he do for a living? When did you meet him? With Pero Tro ... -"

She broke in impatiently. "What use can the answer be to these questions? You cannot send this information."

"Did Sesnik find out anything?"

"What could he find out?" She was busy making Babette

comfortable in the armchair, borrowing Burton's overcoat to use as a rug. "There was nothing but hysteria at the opera."

"Where have you been since? You haven't taken all this time getting here."

"It is not important where we have been. But in the streets people are saying crazy things. What has really happened?"

Burton began to repeat what he had learned, using French for Babette's benefit, but Anna interrupted him.

"Speak English. I will tell her what she needs to know. I wish to spare her."

"Why is she so upset?"

"She is emotional." She said it with clinical detachment. "She has had a very terrible experience."

"Tro ..."

"Please!" She cut in sharply. "It is not necessary for her to hear the name."

Babette and Trovic? Looking swiftly back, he saw that he might have reached the conclusion without prompting, but now he checked the inclination to accept it too readily. Anna's concern for Trovic had been apparent more than once.

He said, "You heard the broadcast?"

"Yes. A prepared record. It is no proof that any particular person is at Radio House."

"They hold the House."

"And the power has been cut off. Do they hold anything else?"

He again started to tell her what he knew, and this time she listened without interrupting. Babette sat in the armchair as if she were numb in body and mind. She watched Anna and Burton, but there was no understanding in her eyes. Anna brought her tea and forced her to drink it. Then, standing over her, with a hand on her shoulder, she gave her part of Burton's story. There was little in it, but Babette was in no state to hear anything. Burton went in to the outer office and got himself some tea. When he returned, Anna was on her knees with her arms round Babette. "It will be all right, my dear," she was saying. "My dear one. My dove."

It would be all right! Maybe.

"I'll go down and try to find a cab," he said. "The thing to do is to get you both home."

"No." Anna stopped him. "I wish her to be with me, and I must be here. I have to know what happens. If things are restored, the agency messages will come in. If not, we will see something from here. If it is true that the Army has risen, there can be little resistance."

"But you can't stay here all night. Babette's in no state . . ."

"She will soon be asleep. There was something in the tea. It was the only way to help her."

"Yes. I see." And if things got really serious, all you had to do was put a little more of something in the tea. Your life was in your handbag. Till Saturday, he reminded himself. Then Anna could be free.

Babette was lying back with closed eyes. "It won't be too comfortable for her in that chair," he said.

"She has been used to less comfort," Anna said. "I know. We worked together many times."

"But she is just a child."

"She is young. Yes."

He went to the window. It came to him then that the murder of Riecke would wash out all the remaining events of the anniversary week. There would be no ceremony at Ranawitz on Saturday; no nine-o'clock train from the Alexis Station. The police would clamp down on everything. You would need a permit, signed and countersigned, to cross the road. Unless, of course, the rising succeeded. Then, maybe, many things would be different.

The tower of Radio House stood out darkly against a glow of reflected light on the low clouds. He imagined that all the approaches to the building were controlled by troops and police. Beyond the line of mounted police halfway down to the quay, the wide street was empty except for a few official cars. Another line reached across the traffic roundabout by the Alexis Bridge. Crowds stood behind the cordons in front of Radio House, waiting. Other people stood behind lighted windows, waiting. Far away across the river a trolley car sparked, breaking the darkness with vivid flashes. Life still moved out there. Only in the centre, at the axial point of government, was there this deadly stillness.

Anna came to his side. "She is asleep."

"You need to sleep yourself."

"No. I must know what happens. In the morning I must try to go to my father, if you will permit it. He will be lost and angry and helpless, and very grieved."

"I will permit it." He reached for her hand to press it reassuringly. It was cold and unresponsive, but she did not withdraw it. He realised that she was unaware of his touch.

"Listen!" she whispered sharply. "Do you hear?"

He raised the window again. Far away to the north a train whistled. Then he heard another sound, a steady mechanical clatter. He closed the window. Yesterday's parade would have made him familiar with the sound if he had not heard it before.

They waited side by side at the window and saw a squadron of medium tanks come into view and pass down the street towards Radio House. The Army was now ready to deal with things.

# XXIV

Soon after dawn there was a spatter of rifle fire and the police down at the Alexis Bridge began to push the crowd farther back. A second burst of firing was followed by a long pause. Ten minutes, fifteen minutes. Burton was restive. He wanted to get down into the street, but the police would turn him back, and from the window he could at least see something of what was going on. He could see the crowd scattering, running towards the bridge and along the quays. He could see the police falling back, seeking cover. Next, the rumbling of caterpillar treads reached him, and one of the tanks clattered into position on the street corner and swung its gun on to Radio House.

He knew then that it was all up with the men inside the building. The Army had failed them. The guns were pointed at the rebels, not at the government, and it was obvious that an ultimatum had been delivered.

Anna began to sob quietly. She was near the end of her endurance. "The fools!" she said. "The poor mad fools! Why did they have to do it?" Another burst of defiant fire broke in on her question. It was the answer to the ultimatum, and the army officer in charge of the operation wasted no time. The tank gun fired and a cloud of dust flew up in the entrance to the building. The second round smashed the heavy metal doors ajar. A third flung aside one of the doors and the improvised barricade behind it. There was a moment's silence, then a smoke canister landed in the road near the entrance. It was followed by two or three more, mortared from a tank Burton could not see. There was a stiff breeze and the smoke screen did not remain thick for very long; but it was enough. As the tanks began to fire their machine guns at the windows from which the rebel fire had been coming, uniformed men with gas masks darted into the smoke with tear-gas projectors in their hands. Chips of masonry flew from the window embrasures as the tanks put in burst after burst of covering fire. Then the men with gas masks returned. A gust of wind thinned the smoke sufficiently for Burton to see the entrance again. Suddenly a man ran down the steps from it with his hands to his face. A burst from a machine pistol got him before he was halfway across the road and he pitched forward and rolled on the cobbles. Troops, working along from a flank, were ready to assault. They tossed in grenades and, as they exploded, went in after them. After a while there was silence. Then an army truck moved from the Breclin Quay followed by an ambulance. There was a sound of fire engines.

Burton said, "Try the Propaganda Ministry again." All through the night they had been attempting to telephone one government department or another, but always the answer had been that no outside calls were being accepted. The official news agency was similarly immobilised. At three o'clock Burton had gone out with the intention of reaching someone in authority, but had been unable to get past the first police line. There was nothing to do but keep on using the telephone, although it was becoming more and more difficult to get the overworked exchange when the automatic system failed to function.

Anna was a long time over her latest attempt. She came from the instrument shaking her head.

"We must wait for the radio," she said. "Perhaps there will be something coming through before long."

Burton switched on the set. Babette was still sleeping, sprawled in the chair. Anna looked as if she might collapse at any minute, but it was no use trying to do anything with her. He had given up. He followed her when she crossed the room to the window.

The people in the street were dispersing, and already the police had reduced the area under control. Someone had removed the body down by the bridge.

Burton went back to the telephone and dialled. He dialled one department after another but there was still no end to the silence.

Anna stood by him, waiting to take over if any linguistic difficulty arose. When he looked up at her, he saw tears in her eyes.

"Why don't you sit down?" he said.

She sat down, and immediately sprang up again. A crackling sound from the radio was followed by the familiar tuning signal. After a minute the voice of a regular announcer came over the air, and Anna translated as he spoke.

"This is the National Broadcasting Service. The insurrection is over. The leader, Andreas Nimsky, alias Pero Trovic, was killed while resisting arrest. The full programme of this service will be resumed when repairs have been effected at the transmitting station. The next news broadcast will be at nine hours."

She faltered over the last words, and Burton feared that now the collapse would come. He gripped her hand. "I'm sorry, Anna," he said. "I can't tell you how sorry." She shook her head and began to speak, brokenly, a little incoherently.

"We are not always responsible. It is the way we have lived that is to blame. It is hard for me that this end had to be so pitiful and futile. Andreas was my brother's best friend, and because of that he was my friend. We three worked always together in the days of the occupation. It is hard for me; it is harder for Babette. She loved Andreas; they were to have been married, but I always feared that she would never be happy with him."

She paused, meeting his gaze. "I must tell you this now because he used you for his purposes. That was his way. He used everybody. He had no love, except for his plans. The war destroyed him. He had not the strength to find his way back. He became a fanatic, and we always feared his madness. I loved him as a comrade, but what can I feel for him now, after last night? The poor old man he murdered was once his friend and leader. Those others, too. And the men who followed him. I begged him that there should be no bloodshed, and he promised me. He promised Babette, too. I helped him when he was in danger. My father gave him shelter, and now I am afraid of the consequences. I do not think he was traced to Tolnitz, but I cannot be sure."

"Anna, dear Anna, don't you see that this life here is impossible for you?"

She shook her head. "More than ever it is necessary for me to stay with my father."

"Then I'll have to get both of you out of the country."

Again she shook her head. "I must go to Tolnitz as soon as you can spare me. Meanwhile, I had better take Babette to her home. I will have to tell her about Andreas when we get there. By now it may be possible to find a cab."

"I'll look after the cab. You'd better see if you can wake her."

# XXV

When they were gone, he at last got a response from the Propaganda Ministry. Agency flashes had already been sent out to the world. Individual messages would be accepted by the censorship after eleven o'clock. Approved photographs would be available to the foreign press within twenty-four hours.

Burton looked up at the clock that ticked out Eastern standard time. Before there was any hope of getting a message through the censor, the last edition would have gone to bed. Anyway, New York had had the news flashes, and there would have been a full obituary of President Riecke waiting in the morgue, with pictures galore, including some of Settembrini's best efforts.

There was no hurry, but Burton started on his job without delay. Now that everything had ended happily for the regime, a good deal of latitude would be permitted, and he might spread himself a bit on his eyewitness account of the assassination. It was a good story, and he had most of it down on paper before Anna returned.

She had not been long. "Babette was calm," she said. "I suppose she knew it could have had no other end. But she will mourn. She will mourn terribly."

"Yes. I suppose so." He was remote for the moment, the newspaper man on the job, the protective armour in position. "Stand by for that broadcast, will you? Then you can get in touch with the university. Have them send round a reliable man. Tell them we don't want a police spy."

She stood by and translated while he made notes. When the reliable man came from the university, he turned out to be the one who had previously presented himself on Sesnik's recommendation.

For a moment Burton's lips tightened. Then he laughed.

"All right," he said. "I'll give you two days' trial. If you get me arrested, you're fired. All you have to do is translate the flimsies as they come in."

"Flimsies, sir?" The young man looked worried.

"Explain to him, Anna. Then you can get off. Phone me when you return to town. And make it soon, or I'll start looking for you."

She came to the inner room a minute later.

"The boy's all right," she told him. "Are you sure you can spare me?"

"Sure. You're quite useless." He got up from his desk. "I don't know what I'm going to do without you."

"Then I shall stay."

"I mean at the end of the week, when you've gone for good."

She hesitated and he saw the trouble in her eyes. Then she turned away wearily.

"You ought to get some sleep," he told her.

"I shall. At Tolnitz."

"Give my greetings to your father. Tell him I'll be coming out to see him. Tell him everything is going to be all right."

"Why do you worry yourself? You have no responsibility for us."

He held out his hand to take hers. He felt the warmth of her hand responding to his clasp. Then, she was in his arms, her forehead pressed against his shoulder. She held tightly to him till the telephone rang in the outer office. He kissed her gently and took her to the door.

"I'll take the call," he told her. "You get some rest now. Come back this evening and we'll have dinner together. There's a lot I want to say to you." She smiled tremulously at him as she went.

It was Sesnik on the line. "I would like to take you to lunch today," he said. "Will you please wait for me at your office?"

There was something of the imperial edict in it. Burton sat staring at the half-typed sheet in his machine, but he was not thinking of Sesnik. The new man brought in flimsy after flimsy with translation attached till there was quite a pile on the desk.

"Are they all right, Mr. Burton?" he asked.

Burton nodded. "They're all right. Everything's fine. What's your name?"

"Wenzl, sir."

"Yes, I remember. Well, Wenzl, how would you like to be President of this great and prosperous country? Just say the word and I'll try to fix it for you."

Wenzl moved away a foot or two. "Perhaps I do not understand, sir?"

"Perhaps you don't. Keep up the good work."

Burton shook himself, and got back to his job. The story was simple enough as he pieced it together from the radio broadcast and the official reports. It was much as he had already figured it out; a story of pitifully inept fanaticism. Destroy the tyrant, broadcast the news, and the whole country would rise! That was the argument and the error.

The timing had been better than the conception. At the moment the bomb was thrown, both Radio House and the transmitting station on the outskirts of the capital were attacked, and a few minutes later Trovic and his helper at the opera joined the party at Radio House. Here complete control had been established, but at the transmitter things went badly for the rebels. A loyal worker managed to throw a switch and cause a temporary breakdown. Repairs were made, transmission was resumed, and then came a counterattack by a strong force of militia. It was successful, but not before more damage was done to the transmitter. Sealed off by the police and with no knowledge of what was happening elsewhere, the party in Radio House waited through the night for the military help that had been promised. Here again easy assumptions had led to overconfidence. Once a move was made, revolt would run like a flame through the Army. But the plans of a certain Colonel Beritic had been betrayed at the last moment. The colonel and a number of other officers had been placed under arrest, and no move could be made. The men and youths in Radio House had nothing to wait for but the end, and they took it with desperate courage when it came.

"There were no survivors." Burton tapped out the words, ripped the sheet from the machine, and took his message to the censor's office. He was utterly weary then, and it seemed to him that the whisky at the Metropole was better than nothing. He felt tired enough to have been up for two nights rather than one. When he sat down at a table in the Metropole lounge, he was afraid he would fall asleep; but the whisky revived him, and then Attridge and some of the other men dropped in and they began to talk over the events of the night.

It was late when he got back to the office, and Sesnik was waiting for him. Sesnik was very spruce in his bulbous way. He wore a black tie in recognition of the national calamity, but there was nothing solemn about him. He beamed. He was happy. Perhaps he did not like presidents.

"I see," he said, "that you have taken young Wenzl under your wing after all. I am glad of it. He is a worthy boy. I knew his mother very well. A handsome and courtly woman. The father was no good. A scoundrel, a collaborator, and in the pay of the British. He tried to escape. He had reached the last barrier of barbed wire when he trod on a bomb. It is very, very difficult to escape."

"That's what your friend Trovic must have thought," Bur-ton retorted. "It seems that he didn't even try. You must have been rather surprised, the way he turned up last night."

"My dear friend, I am never surprised." The comical mouth looked more comical. "When I make myself a theory, I recognise that there is always an alternative. Sometimes I make three and even four theories, so I am never surprised."

"But you don't win much money if you back every horse on the card."

This was immensely funny to Sesnik. He quaked and wobbled. "The money does not matter. The important thing is to hold the winning ticket."

"Trovic is dead. Does that pay a dividend?"

"There is another race on the card. Let us go to lunch, my dear Burton. I am hungry. I had no breakfast. I will take you to a small place where we can get an excellent shish kebab with ladies' fingers."

Burton had had nothing but tea and whisky. The kebab was really excellent, served sizzling hot on the skewer. Sesnik talked of food and cookery with abandon. He was a trencherman. "One evening you must come to my apartment and I will cook for you. I am a modest practitioner, I lay no claims to the cordon bleu, but what I do, I do well. As soon as the successor to Riecke is appointed, I will send you an invitation."

"Who is to be the successor?"

"Who can say? I think you have already had an instruction that there is to be no newspaper speculation."

"Sure, but I'm not asking as a newspaper man."

"Again I must say I do not know. Perhaps it will be Monsieur Varlein. He is not too badly hurt. A broken jaw and a gashed thigh. He hurled himself down just in time."

"You think Varlein's a good man?"

"It is a matter for the Supreme Council. They will present the candidate to the people and ask for a vote. Now you must have some Turkish coffee. No better coffee is made in Istanbul."

"Sorry. I can't stand the stuff. I'll take a glass of tea."

Sesnik made no further attempt to talk to the barbarian about the things that matter. Instead he produced a much used wrist watch with a chromium case and laid it on the table in front of Burton.

"Can you identify that?" he inquired.

Burton could. He said, "It looks like a watch. Cheap Swiss, I suppose."

"It is Sokolny's watch."

"Now you come to mention it, it does seem familiar. But one never takes much notice of another person's watch."

"I do." The moon face wore its most expansive smile. "For instance, my dear Burton, I notice that you have a new brown strap on your watch. When I first met you, it was a black strap."

"Extraordinary!" Burton smiled back. "I suppose that's the sort of gift that makes you a policeman."

"But why have you changed your strap? That is something I cannot tell."

"No? What about a daring guess? The black strap was worn nearly through. I didn't want to lose my watch, so I bought a new strap. But it can't possibly interest you."

"It might interest me if I knew where you bought it."

"Good heavens, Sesnik, don't tell me I've been patronising a receiver of stolen property. Has somebody been misappropriating the state supply of watch straps? I bought it in a most respectable shop on the Breclin Quay, close to the Alexis Bridge."

"Ah!" Sesnik sighed deeply and sipped his abominable coffee. "The shop of Emil Dovinye?"

"I think that was the name. What's the mystery?"

"It was in the same shop that we found Sokolny's watch." "So I murdered Sokolny and sold his watch to Dovinye!" Burton laughed and Sesnik joined in, spilling the thick muddy coffee over a fat finger. "The fact is that Sokolny recommended the watchmaker to me," Burton went on. "I was in need of a new strap."

"So you said. What puzzles me is how Sokolny's watch came into the possession of Dovinye."

"Now don't help me." Burton frowned. "Let me try my hand at deduction. Sokolny's watch broke down and he took it to Dovinye to be repaired."

"A very interesting theory. The only thing that's wrong with it is that Sokolny was dead. It is possible, in a certain kind of romance, to have him walk out of the mortuary and take his watch to Dovinye, but there was no watch on him when the police arrived at your office."

"The answer is that it was already in the shop."

"No, my dear Burton. It was taken to Dovinye after his death. There was blood on the strap, Sokolny's blood."

"So that's the theory! What about the alternative?"

"Have you an alternative?"

"For the blood on the strap? Yes. Sokolny had been having some teeth out."

Sesnik stared, his mouth forming an O. His hand descending smacked his little coffee cup into the saucer. Burton enjoyed the effect of his hit for a moment, then rubbed in the salt.

"It's easy enough to check," he said. "Just ask Dovinye when he received the watch from Sokolny."

"Dovinye is dead."

"Dead? He seemed in good health when I bought my strap. It's very sudden isn't it?"

"Very sudden. Like Sokolny. Like Riecke."

"You're not linking them up?" Burton introduced a note of protest. "You surely don't think "Sesnik cut in. "I'm trying to find out why Sokolny was murdered. He knew Trovic, the assassin. The death of Riecke had been planned."

"I knew Trovic. Does that make me guilty of anything?"

"Anna Maras knew Trovic."

"She knew that he was doing a job for me. If it comes to that, Sokolny's acquaintance with him was much longer."

"Trovic was in the Resistance movement during the war. So was Anna."

"What does that prove?"

"Nothing." Sesnik shrugged, making quite an effort of it. "I am trying to trace the history of certain figures in the Resistance. It is difficult because it was all so clandestine. It is difficult, but I shall succeed in the end. I am a very patient man, Mr. Burton. Very, very patient. Where is Anna today, by the way?"

"She was at the office all night, standing by. I sent her home to get some rest." He hesitated, then decided that frankness was the best policy. "To Tolnitz. She was troubled about her father. The family was so friendly with President Riecke."

"Yes." Sesnik nodded. "That presents us with one of the anomalies. Anna would never have done anything to harm the unfortunate Riecke. There was that little unexpected scene at the saluting base. Quite touching. I wonder what Monsieur Vulcan thought of it. After what has happened, there is likely to be a purge of undesirable elements. The prospect is quite terrifying. More so to some than to others. There are threads in our political fabric that get rather tangled, and the innocent threads become mixed with the guilty. Will you have some more coffee?" He beamed again, then expressed by gesture that he was annoyed with himself. "My apologies," he said. "I see you are drinking tea."

# XXVI

No call came from Anna. Ever since he had left Sesnik, Burton had been worried about her, and towards evening his anxiety became acute. Sesnik was suspicious of everybody who had come into contact with Trovic, suspicious of Burton himself as well as of Anna. If he discovered that Anton Maras had given shelter to Trovic, anything might happen. Maras would be arrested. Anna, too. Or they would be held for examination. Held for weeks, perhaps, till they broke down. Sesnik had nothing to be afraid of now that Maras no longer had the protection of Riecke. And Maras was a sick man, with no physical endurance. The ordeal would kill him.

Burton tried to check the riot of horrors in his mind. He had a job to do and for the most part it demanded full attention. All day, news items, facts, theories, announcements came pouring in, and everything had to be considered. There was little to add to the first story he had sent to New York, but each follow-up message had a weight of material behind it and it was necessary to keep on the alert. A highly important statement might be released at any moment. Meanwhile there were the arrangements for the lying in state and the programme for the funeral, which was to be held on Sunday.

During the afternoon Burton made a round of the government offices, talking to the higher-ups, trying to get a line on the likely successor to Riecke. Varlein was the name most often mentioned, but some questioned whether he would give up his position of Party

Secretary. He was already the most powerful man in the land. Why should the maker of Presidents wish to become President?

Burton shrugged. His interest was purely objective. He didn't know any of the answers. He went to Settembrini to see if he had any pictures of Varlein.

"I suppose Saturday's trip is off," he said.

"If the Ranawitz ceremony is cancelled, there will be no nine-o'clock train," Settembrini answered. "I am not yet giving up hope. Ranawitz is an unbroken tradition, and something apart from the celebrations here. 'The government will be reluctant to cancel. Varlein I am sure would object. It is his pet show. Here is a nice picture of him among the ruins. Varlein and a broken column. Two pieces of granite against the sky. My clouds are rather nice, I think."

"To the devil with your clouds."

Settembrini smiled. "Besides, I am putting out the suggestion, through certain agents, that Ranawitz offers a wonderful opportunity for a memorial service to Riecke. The day of national mourning. Another name added to the honour roll of martyrs. It is a pity Varlein's jaw was fractured. No one else could be so eloquent on the theme. He hated Riecke."

"Varlein doesn't interest me. I want to know when you're going to get Anna Maras out of this country."

"I still hope it will be on Saturday. That is all I can tell you. We must wait and see. Meanwhile, you should be patient."

The advice was hard to take. Leaving the photographer, Burton turned into the vestibule of the Propaganda Ministry to use a phone.

"Wenzl, is there any message from Miss Maras?"

"No, sir. Not yet."

"How are you getting on?"

"Quite good, I hope, sir."

"Keep it up. You'll have to work late tonight if Miss Maras doesn't get back."

"I will be proud to, sir."

Attridge was coming up the steps. "Heard the news from the Supreme Council?" he inquired. "The meeting to name the new President is fixed for Friday. The funeral, baked meats, etcetera." He laughed. "By the way, what's your pretty secretary been up to? Crossing the street in the wrong place?"

Burton felt as if something had hit him. He wondered if Attridge had noticed his start. Striving to show nothing more, he said casually, "What are you talking about?"

"Sorry if I gave you a shock." Attridge laughed again. "I didn't think you were the jumpy sort. After last night I guess we're all a bit worn out."

"Would you mind explaining about Anna Maras?"

"Surely you know? I was only joking, anyway. I was down at the Police Judiciary when they brought her in. I mean it looked like that. Maybe she was on some errand for you."

"She's with her father at Tolnitz. You must be mistaken."

"Mistaken about Anna Maras? Don't be crazy, Burton! I wasn't five yards away from her. This car drives up just as I come through the swing door. There are a couple of plainclothes footmen along and they take her through that little green door on the street level. Don't tell me she really is under arrest!"

"What time was it?"

"About half-after three. I had just come . . ." He stared at Burton, leaving the sentence unfinished. "That reminds me. There's talk that your man Sokolny bumped himself off the other night. There's also talk that this fellow Trovic did jobs for you."

"Maybe there's talk that I was asking where I could buy a bomb?"

"Sure, but old Gregor thought that was just one of your wisecracks. Wait a minute. Don't be in such a hurry. I want to know ---------- "

Burton was out of earshot. It was six when he entered the Police Judiciary building. He asked to see Sesnik and was told it was impossible. He scribbled a few lines on a scrap of paper and requested that it be taken to Sesnik. He was told that the commissioner had left the building and would not be available till the next day.

He became noisily insistent and they sent for an interpreter. He made more noise and they produced Sesnik's secretary, a pale young man with large spectacles.

"Where is Anna Maras?" he demanded. "What have you done with her?"

"Who is Anna Maras?" inquired the secretary politely.

"He knows damn well who she is," Burton shouted at the interpreter. "She was brought in here at three-thirty. If Sesnik isn't responsible, who is?"

The pale secretary shrugged his shoulders and began to walk away. Burton grabbed him and swung him round roughly. In a split second four pairs of hands were laid on Burton.

"You will please wait," the interpreter advised him gently. "The results of instantaneous inquiries will be promulgated."

Burton closed his eyes tightly for a moment. Nothing was to be gained by making a fool of himself.

The interpreter followed the secretary. After ten minutes he returned. It was quite true, he said, that the young lady had visited the Judiciary. She had been invited to do so by Deputy Commissioner Gröte, who was assisting Commissioner Sesnik in certain inquiries. The young lady had left the building at four-seventeen.

"You mean she was released?" Burton wanted to get it quite clear.

"Released?" The interpreter was puzzled. "I do not comprehend. To be released, you have firstly to be arrested. Miss Maras did not come here to be a prisoner."

"Where is she now?"

"That we do not know. It is not our business. Perhaps she is where it gives her pleasure to be. This is a free country."

A free country for the police, perhaps! Out in the street again he wondered if they were still shadowing him. It was some days since he had made any tests, and he was not disposed to make any now. They could follow him as long as they liked. It did not bother him any longer. If they were following him tonight, all they would learn was that he was looking for Anna Maras.

He found a cab and was driven to her lodging. He learned that she had come home during the morning, had changed her clothes and gone out again. That was the last anyone had seen of her.

His next call was on Babette. If Anna had been released after questioning, she might have had occasion to talk to her friend, but the dancer shook her head. Anna had not been back.

On the way down the stairs, Burton had the idea that he was wasting time. She might be waiting for him at the office. He ordered his driver to take him there, but there was no Anna at the end of the journey; not even a telephone message to say she was coming.

He forced himself to deal with the news that had come in, but all the time he worried about Anna. He thought of the last time he had searched for her. He had covered the same ground, but tonight there was a difference. A good deal had happened in the interim. A great deal.

Wenzl was at his elbow, waiting for the cable. Wenzl was a nice boy. Helpful.

"Shall I take it to the censor, sir?" he asked.

"Yes." Burton gave him instructions. "Take an hour off and get something to eat. If I'm out when you return, wait for me."

He leaned back in his chair, trying to think, but the one thought chased round perpetually in his head. Anna was in danger. He had to do something to get her out of it, but there was nothing he could do. He closed his eyes and felt his head nodding. He sprang from the chair, shaking away the sleep. He hunted in the top drawer of his desk through the accumulation of odds and ends, erasers, discarded pens, aspirin, a million pencils, a pocket compass, quinine, a worn pinochle deck, benzedrine . . .

He swallowed a tablet and went to the filter for water. There was a psychological effect in advance of the physical. He felt safe from sleep already. Soon he might be able to figure something out. All he could figure at the moment was that the police were probably lying and were holding Anna. If she were free she would have communicated with him by now.

Unless she had gone into hiding.

Perhaps she had gone to Tolnitz earlier in the day. Perhaps the police had followed her there to pick her up.

Anton Maras might know something. He might know what to do; might still have some influence that he could use in his daughter's favour. If she should be safe after all, there was still the escape in prospect, and Burton needed to see old Maras about that; to persuade him to accompany Anna, or, if he wouldn't do that, to write a letter for delivery to Anna.

The telephone rang. It was Babette. She wanted to know if there was any word from Anna. "I am frightened," she said.

That made two. He closed the office, found another cab and went to Tolnitz.

When he arrived he told the driver to wait and stood looking about him for a moment. This was his third visit and he felt that he knew the tall pines and the wide-branched cedars behind the high wall, though tonight there was no moon and he saw them only as dark shapes.

Once more he pushed at the broken gate, squeezed through the opening, and walked up the overgrown path. Once more he saw the flat-walled house across the ruined garden, but dimly tonight in the pale light of the stars. The place was in darkness. He peered through the slats of the closed jalousies, but no light burned in the study. The bell rang loudly when he pressed the button at the side of the door. He waited, then rang again. He remembered that Maras was slow in movement. He listened intently, but no sound came to him from behind the closed door. Far away to the north he heard the echoing throb of a train. Then a car droned along the road from the direction of the city. Near at hand it seemed to slow down, but it passed the gate and went on.

Burton rang the bell a third time and waited. No one came. Now he took hold of the handle and turned it. The door opened. From the threshold he called loudly.

"Doctor Maras!"

He advanced into the hall and repeated the call, but no response came from the dark house. The cold made him shiver. He flicked on his lighter and held it up in front of him. The door of the study, the only room he had entered on his previous visit, was closed.

Once more he called. "Doctor Maras! Professor!" The wick of the lighter burned low for lack of fuel. He rapped on the study door and opened it. He expected the warmth of the lived-in room, but tonight there was no change from the icy air of the hall.

"Doctor Maras!"

Perhaps the old man was asleep in his chair. Burton found the light switch and turned it. The study came up out of darkness: the worn red carpet, the great desk, the books in the dark cases, the table with the bottles of liquor and glasses. The silver tea urn was in its place, but there was no small blue flame beneath it to keep the water hot.

Burton crossed to the stove and found that it was cold. And there was another change. The desk that had been a litter of books and papers had been tidied. The books had been restored to shelves, the papers were piled neatly.

"Doctor Maras!" Back in the hall he shouted the name again.

It was no use. There was no one to hear.

He switched on more lights. He opened doors and looked in the rooms on the ground floor; musty, unused rooms with curtains drawn behind closed shutters.

Now he was convinced that the police had come here and taken Anton Maras away; that they were holding both Anna and her father in the cells of the Judiciary building. They had gone through the old man's papers, had found some incriminating letter, a message in the hand of Trovic, perhaps. Perhaps they had also taken the precious book, the labour of years, to be used in evidence before it was destroyed.

Burton hesitated in the cold hall. He told himself bitterly that he had nothing more to do here, yet he could not bring himself to go. He walked to the front door and hesitated again. He stared at the door wondering why it had been left open. It was not like the police to be so careless. When they took a man away they were usually careful to seal up his rooms.

There was something odd about it. It might be a trap. But for whom? Fugitives who might seek help from the professor?

He switched off the lights, and went cautiously up the stairs, listening after every few steps. If he walked into an ambush, he had a legitimate excuse for being in the house, and Sesnik, whatever his suspicions, would be able to do nothing about it.

He called the name of Maras again so that there could be no doubt about the open nature of his visit. Then, as he reached the landing, he halted abruptly, peering forward. A light showed dimly at the bottom of a closed door.

Silently he moved to the door and listened. No sound. The light at his feet was unsteady. He opened the door a fraction of an inch and listened again. He widened the opening and looked in. The light came from four candles in silver sticks placed on chairs, one at each corner of a narrow bed. The flames flickered a little in the draught, throwing shadows on the ceiling and light on the wax-grey face of Anton Maras, who lay rigid under a white coverlet.

Burton stepped forward and lifted one of the candlesticks, but before he looked closely he knew that Maras was dead. The face was that of a very old man, deeply lined. But there was serenity there now.

A sound from below made his heart jolt wildly. The front door was opened and closed again. He moved to the landing as a light was switched on in the hail. He waited tensely, straining to listen.

Someone was coming up the stairs.

# XXVII

It was Anna. She did not see him in the gloom of the landing and he called to her, almost shouting her name in his relief. She halted at the top of the stairs and peered.

"I've been trying to reach you by telephone," she said in a curiously matter-of-fact tone. "I had to walk to the post office. It is more than a mile. I left Marfa Baranu here. She is the woman who looked after my father. No doubt she has gone down to the village to get her husband's supper. She will return. I am sorry there was no one in the house to --"

"Anna!" he said. She took a step forward as he moved towards her; but she went on speaking coldly and clearly as if no emotion could ever touch her again.

"Did you come by car?" she said. "I walked across the field and along the lane by the riverbank. It is shorter that way. Wenzl told me you had gone out."

"Anna!"

Her hands reached towards him and he held her tightly. She began to cry, and he knew suddenly that these were her first tears for her father. He tried to think of words that might give her comfort, but there were none. He waited in silence, holding her in his arms. After a while she raised her head.

"You must go back to the city," she said.

"There is plenty of time," he answered. "The car will wait. I must know what happened and what you will do. I heard that you were taken to the Judiciary. I tried to see Sesnik."

She shivered. "It is warmer in the study," she said. "We will go down stairs."

There, she switched on an electric fire, and, kneeling before it, told him what had happened.

Anton Maras had been crushed by the news of the assassination. All the differences he had had with Riecke had become unimportant; the affection had endured. He had pitied Riecke although he had condemned his vanity. He had seen him as a bemused old man, weakly accepting the illusion of power, persuading himself that he was serving his people. If Anton Maras had stood beside him, Riecke might have had the will to resist the ambitions of Varlein, but Maras had opposed him. He had seen Riecke's acceptance of office as an act of betrayal. But the end had been brought about by another act of betrayal. That of Trovic.

He had not understood Trovic. He had known fanaticism, had realised the insane lengths to which it might be carried, but had not seen Trovic as a fanatic. Anna and Babette, too, had been deceived. Trovic had acted heroically in helping refugees to get out of the country; his friends had known of his work and the grave risks he ran. When Sesnik began his inquiries, Anna believed that Trovic had really crossed the frontier near Kazyos, but on the night of Swan Lake at the opera she had learned that he was still in the country and had gone at once to find him, to tell him what she knew and warn him about Sesnik.

While she had talked with him, she had had a vague suspicion that something was being prepared, but no hint of the truth had entered her mind. At the worst she had feared some sort of demonstration at one or other of the anniversary celebrations; had feared it because of the danger that Trovic would be in. And Babette had pleaded with him to leave the country, to follow one of the routes he had planned successfully for others. Then, when she could, she would join him.

Trovic's answer had been that he had work to do.

"He came here, to Tolnitz," Anna told Burton. "He had been hidden here before, and again he asked my father to help him. It was from this house that he went out last night."

She had risen from in front of the electric fire and crossed to the desk where Anton Maras had worked. She stood in front of the chair and looked down at the desk.

"Can you understand what my father must have felt?" She hesitated. "Perhaps it is not easy for you to realise all our confusion. It has not been happy for us since the war. There are always loyalties that cut across other loyalties, and it is difficult to know what is best for our country. My father was a very unhappy man in this confusion. He talked a lot. He talked sometimes loudly, but he had not the strength or the hardness to make a clear course for himself. I know how gentle and kindly he was and how he felt for his old friend Riecke. You see, don't you? If you have the ruthlessness of a fanatic, you can make the way simple enough."

"If you want to make it short."

She looked at him across the desk. "Trovic never saw the end. He could only see the argument. That had to be followed, no matter what happened. He loved Babette. He revered my father. He killed him as surely as he killed Uncle Riecke. . . . I am very tired."

For a moment she leaned forward, her hands pressing on the desk, then she sat down in the chair. Burton came round behind her. "Anna, my dear!"

She took his hand and held it tightly. Her eyes were dry again, staring across the room.

"It's over now," he said. "There's nothing more for you here."

"That is what he told me. We were together in this room. He said no word of Trovic. There was not even the mention of the name, but I knew how deeply hurt he was and how he mourned for Riecke. 'You must leave me now,' he said. 'I am at the end of my life, but you are young. You must live for me. You must go away.' "

Burton felt her grip tighten on his hand.

"I told him that I would never leave him," she went on. "Now, more than ever, I wished to stay with him. He was angry with me. He said I must obey. I was to speak to you and ask for your help. I insisted that I would not leave him. Then the police came to take me to the Judiciary. A man named Gröte asked me about Trovic. Whatever he suspected, it was clear he knew nothing, and certainly there was no suspicion that Trovic had ever been in this house. The police were following up the old story. I had worked with Trovic in the resistance movement; possibly I had kept up the acquaintance. Gröte was polite. They were all polite. But they have not finished with me. When they could get nothing out of me, they brought me back here in their car. Back here . . ."

She paused as if she had need to gather her strength. "I found my father upstairs. He was lying across his bed. He was dead. I closed his eyes."

Her voice carried that suggestion of remoteness again. She was looking at something far away.

"I know why he died. He wanted to set me free. He was hurt, he had no hope left, and he was a hindrance to me. That is how he saw it. Perhaps he thought the police would hold me, that they would return to fetch him. All the day he had been full of fear and uncertainty and anxiety for me, and the solution was always at hand for him; an overdose of that drug."

"You brought the doctor, of course?" Burton had no doubt that she was right, but he wanted confirmation.

"In Tolnitz we live among friends. That is why it was possible for Trovic to come here. The doctor is a very old friend. He knows what would follow if a hint of suicide got out after the failure of the revolt, and he knows that my father had no part in the plot. He wants no false assumptions, so he is saying that death was due to a seizure. It may be thought that the shock of Riecke's death was too hard a blow. It is true enough, but I have told you the real cause. If I had not refused to leave him, he would still be alive."

"You must not blame yourself, my dear."

"I am not blaming myself. I am stating a fact. He wished to set me free."

"He wished you to escape to America?"

"Yes." She turned to look at him sadly.

"It is arranged, then. You will go on from Ranawitz on Saturday. I will join you in Vienna as soon as I can get there."

"Saturday?"

He told her what he had planned; confessed that she might have been taken across the frontier against her will. "Now, perhaps, it will be much simpler," he said.

"I want more time," she answered. "There is much to do, and it will not be easy for me. This is my country. I have my roots here and my friends. And there is Babette, who needs me. It is impossible to go so soon."

He argued that there was no time. Gröte would be followed by Sesnik, and Sesnik, suspicious before the revolt, would now be watching her day after day. And Heaven alone knew what the investigation of the Trovic business might not throw up. The pilgrimage to Ranawitz afforded a favourable opportunity that might never recur. Since she could take nothing but a handbag with her, there was no preparation to be made for the journey. If there was anything she could not attend to before Saturday, he would see to it.

Babette?

Very well, he would see to Babette. It might even be possible to get her across the frontier, and it would not be difficult for such a good dancer to make a living. At least he would sponsor her as far as Vienna.

Anna shook her head. "Babette will not go," she asserted positively. "There is nothing but the ballet for her now and nothing will tear her from the theatre. It would be wrong, for her career is here. She will get over Trovic in time. Soon she will be a great ballerina. That will help."

"But there is no career here for you." He argued almost harshly now. "We don't know what is working in Sesnik's mind. I want to get you out of his reach."

She rose from the chair and leaned on the desk again. If she had heard the name of Sesnik, she ignored it. She looked round the study.

"I failed him," she said.

"He had his work to occupy him," Burton reminded her.

"The great testament of Anton Maras," she said at last. "Is that what you mean?"

"Yes." He was puzzled by the bitterness in her voice. "We will have to look after that. Or you will. It's a charge on you now."

"A charge?"

"To do what he would have wished you to do. Once you get the manuscript to America, there will be no difficulty. I know a man in New York who will find the right publisher."

"There's nothing to publish."

"You mean that the book is not finished. But the bulk of the argument is there. You'll be able to supply whatever is missing. Tell the story of the end in a final chapter. It will add to the force of it."

She was looking across the room at a picture on the wall, the painting of a bearded man in some sort of uniform . . . a king or a prophet or some obscure ancestor.

"Don't you see that there's a double reason now for you to get away from this country?" he said. "There's the book's safety as well as yours to be considered."

"There is no book," she said.

"No book?" He stared at her. "Do you mean he destroyed it?"

She opened a drawer of the desk and took out a file of foolscap sheets.

"This is all there ever was of it," she told him. "The first chapter. An examination of the Napoleonic constitution. There are five or six versions and this is the latest, and there's no more in it than he put into a textbook he wrote twenty years ago. There are notes for other chapters; they are quite useless."

"But the bulk of his work? He told me--"

The look in her eyes made him halt.

"Yes, he told you," she repeated. "The truth is that my father did not die today. He died a long time ago. The man who lived in this house was a shadow. He talked of a great book, but he was no longer able to write it. I have told no one but you of this. I do not wish anyone else to know. I remember my father as a great and good man. That is how I wish him to be remembered. There is nothing to be done with this." She threw the file down on the desk. "I shall destroy it with the other papers in the house. Then I shall be free."

He waited, thinking. He said, "Everything necessary can be done by Friday. On Saturday morning you will be on the train for Ranawitz."

She gave no sign that she heard him. Once more she looked round the study. "This place has nothing for me," she said. "He gave me all that I want to keep."

"It will be quite simple," he went on quietly. "You will go on from Ranawitz, and I'll write at once for a transfer. If I don't get it, I'll turn in the job. All you'll have to do is wait in Vienna till I join you."

She turned, reaching towards him, her eyes full of tears. He held her while she wept. He thought then that she would find some peace and come to a decision, and he was right. In the end she gave him her word. She would be guided by him and by her father's wish. She became practical, then. There was little time, but her friends in Tolnitz, the doctor and others, would help her. She would return to town on Friday evening, ready to take the train to Ranawitz on Saturday morning.

# XXVIII

On Thursday afternoon Burton had the news that there would be no train on Saturday morning. The Supreme Council had decided to cancel the proceedings at Ranawitz. The day of grief would be devoted exclusively to the memory of their beloved and heroic President Riecke. Wenzl translated the message as soon as it came in, and again Burton went to Settembrini, this time in desperation, for fears had multiplied in the night.

No obliging doctor could prevent Sesnik from becoming suspicious about the death of Anton Maras, and once the idea of suicide was planted in the official mind, there would be no bounds to the zeal of the investigators. Obstacles might be placed in their way, but somehow they would discover the association of Maras and Trovic. Anna was in grave danger, and, if it cost Burton every penny he had, Settembrini, the escape expert, must be induced to do something about it. Even Saturday might be too late. To wait beyond that day would be to invoke disaster.

The escape expert led his caller gloomily to his inner parlour. Burton checked on the threshold when he saw that there was a third party present.

"The bad news about Ranawitz has reached me," Settembrini said. "Already two clients are demanding their money back."

Burton threw an apprehensive glance in the direction of the third party. Settembrini murmured a casual introduction. The name sounded something like Karazelos, Zeno Karazelos. "You need have no qualms," Settembrini added. "Zeno was to have been in charge of the party. He is experienced. In Athens he worked as a guide for a distinguished travel agency. Here he is the valued servant of the State Tourist Bureau. He has been of great help to me for a long time. I hated the thought that I would be deprived of his services by his own escape, but now it seems that "

"Enough," Zeno interrupted in a crackling tone. "You know that the audit will be completed next week. It is impossible for me to return to the office after Saturday."

"With a name like yours, you should be more of a philosopher," Settembrini told him, then turned to Burton. "There is, unfortunately, some money missing from Zeno's department. By a curious coincidence, he left Athens in similar circumstances."

"Let us forget about Athens," said Zeno with dignity. "At present, I have to get out of this unspeakable country. If I had thought for a moment that the train would not run on Saturday, I would not . . ."

"You would not have taken the money."

Karazelos drew himself up and glowered. He was a lean man with a lean head and piercing brown eyes. Burton could easily picture him in the peaked cap of a tourist guide, his predatory nose smelling out the rich arrivals on station platforms and in airport reception halls. His shiny blue suit and pointed brown shoes were almost a livery.

"That is a lie," he said stiffly. "I meant to pay everything back. I will do so. In Vienna the American Express will give me a job. I will save. I will repay. Essentially, I am an honest man."

"The auditors will be pleased to hear it."

"It is you I accuse, Settembrini," said Zeno bitterly. "I advised you from the first that we should use an ordinary, everyday train." He appealed to Burton. "There is always trouble when an amateur tries to run a travel business."

"How could we get a party of more than thirty on to an

ordinary train without causing suspicion?" Settembrini demanded.

"That is no problem to a professional. A bribe here, a bribe there, and all difficulties disappear."

"Perhaps you can bribe Sesnik to lift the ban on the Ranawitz fiesta?" Settembrini said disagreeably.

"Sesnik?" Burton came in with a considerable note of alarm in his question. "What has he got to do with it? The order came from the Supreme Council."

"On the advice of the police," Settembrini asserted. "The department concerned is Sesnik's. They are still hunting the friends of Trovic. It is logical that they do not want any unnecessary movements of people at such a time. Sesnik himself is in a weak position. If he does not make arrests, he may be broken. The bosses will be looking for scapegoats. However much they may congratulate themselves on the murder of Riecke, it is a political necessity to avenge it."

"With Sesnik it is more than a political necessity," the Greek added. "The Minister of Security had made him responsible for Trovic. The Minister is the close personal friend of Halvic, Riecke's chief aide, and tomorrow the Supreme Council will make Halvic the new President."

Burton looked from Karazelos to Settembrini. "But I thought that Varlein's election was assured."

Settembrini shook his head. "That was yesterday. Today the betting is on Halvic. It is Varlein, you remember, who has the broken jaw. In times of crisis it is a disadvantage to have a broken jaw. But, Halvic or Varlein, your friend Sesnik is in a dilemma. I would not like to be one whom he suspects, even if he has no evidence."

Burton felt his scalp tighten. "Listen, Settembrini," he said, "you've got to do something about Anna Maras. She must get out of the country at once."

"What can I do?" Settembrini frowned. "Ask Karazelos. He is

experienced. He is also desperate. If he could get to the frontier, he would run the hazards of the wire and the mines and the sentries, but there is no way he can get to the frontier. Do you think this is a happy day for me? After all the weeks of planning and working and spending. We put all our trust in one train to get our party on the move. Karazelos may criticise our choice of train, but it was inevitable. There was no other way."

"You must find another way," Burton urged him.

"Perhaps you have a suggestion?"

"What about a plane?"

Settembrini shook his head. "We've worked that trick too often. They have guards on them now. Besides, it is always difficult to find a pilot who wants to escape. And at such short notice . . ." He shrugged.

"If it's a matter of bribing someone, I'll find more money. I'll find all you need."

"No. It is impossible. It may take months. The only course now is to wait till things calm down. Then we will carry out our original plan with another train." "How soon?"

"Who knows?" Settembrini shrugged. "It may be a week or ten days. It may be a month or more."

"A week may be too long a time. Anna Maras cannot wait."

"That's too bad. I would help you if I could, Burton, but there's nothing to be done."

"Nothing," Karazelos added tragically, "except to wait for the axe."

The whole city seemed to be waiting for something. A quiet that suggested the Sabbath had settled on the streets that Burton traversed on his way back to the office. Business was at a standstill. Only the shops that dealt in food and drink and other immediate necessities were open, and all premises, open or closed, displayed signs of mourning. Everywhere there were portraits of Riecke with red and black drapes over the frames, and people formed a mile-long queue that inched and shuffled towards the great Hall of the Republic where the dead President lay on his bier. All along the riverbank the queue stretched and grew and grew till it seemed it must reach to the Yalinsky Gate.

Burton stood and watched the line for a moment. These people were moved by more than the desire to be in the show. They were sincere. They wished to pay a last tribute to a man they had revered. Tomorrow they would hail the choice of the Supreme Council and in due course confirm the election of the new President. Halvic . . .

Better the crude, calculating Varlein than the sinister little man whose great contribution to the State had been the creation of the political police.

Burton looked behind him, and a little farther on looked round a second time. He was sure he had been given a respite by Sesnik, but now he was under surveillance again. There was no question of shadowing. He was being followed quite openly, at a distance of less than twenty yards. He felt as if a hand might reach out and grasp him if he turned in the wrong direction.

When he reached the office, Wenzl was working on an agency report. It announced the death from a heart seizure of the distinguished Dr. Anton Maras, and, in a few lines devoted to his career, described him as an old-guard Social Democrat. That was all, except for the information that the funeral would be at Tolnitz the following day.

Burton looked over the rest of the news. It dealt mainly with the arrangements for the Riecke obsequies on Sunday. There was nothing more about the cancellation of the Ranawitz ceremony, but quite a lengthy report on the activities of the police. The ramifications of the Trovic plot had been widespread and many suspects had been arrested. Inquiries were being pursued on the basis of information furnished by a number of the prisoners. The police had succeeded in tracing the movements of Trovic immediately prior to the assassination; important developments were expected. Meanwhile, all movements from the city were under strict control.

There was little to add to the follow-up story that Burton had already lodged with the censor. Burton told Wenzl to take a three-hour break. He himself waited until six o'clock and then walked to his hotel, trailed by the man he had observed during the afternoon. He had scarcely time to turn round in his room when a knock sounded on his door. For a moment he believed that the police had come, but he was wrong. Babette stood in the doorway.

"I waited for you in the foyer," she said. "I had to talk to you, but did not dare to go to your office. I was afraid there might be a man on watch."

He brought her into the room and closed the door.

"I am afraid for Anna," she told him hurriedly in a voice that had a note of panic in it. "We were all called to the opera this afternoon to be questioned. Sesnik was there. He asked me about Anna and Trovic. I denied Trovic, denied everything about him. Sesnik believed me. But he is convinced that Anna had dealings with Trovic. He revealed his mind by the things he asked me. Then he told me the terrible news about Anna's father. He told me as if it were something that he linked with Trovic and President Riecke. If Anna is still at Tolnitz, we must try to reach her."

"Were you followed here?" Burton asked.

"No."

"Are you sure?"

"I am experienced, and I am sure. Otherwise I would not have come here. No one can know that I came to see you."

"Why did you think my office might be watched?"

Babette hesitated. "Sesnik asked me about you, also. He asked me about the night you came with Anna to see me dance in *Swan Lake*. That was the night she went to Trovic and took him to Tolnitz. If they find out that he was at Tolnitz "

She broke off helplessly.

"You had better go home, Babette. There's nothing you can do."

"Will you go to Tolnitz?"

"Yes." He answered confidently, but he felt anything but confident. He could do no more than Babette. He could go to Tolnitz and tell Anna what she already knew. He could assure himself, perhaps, that she was safe enough tonight, but he would find no assurance for tomorrow.

Babette said, "Sesnik frightens me. There is only one way of safety for Anna. She has relations in America. She should go to them."

"What about you?" Burton asked her. "Aren't you afraid of Sesnik?"

"No. He will not discover what Trovic was to me, or even that I knew him. I know what you are thinking, my dear friend, but I am safe and I wish to stay here with my people and my work."

"All right, Babette. If you change your mind before I leave here myself, get in touch with me."

Get in touch with him! He thought it over bitterly when she had gone. Much good it would be now for her to get in touch with Wonder-Boy Burton. Settembrini and his Greek guide couldn't arrange an escape from a paper bag. He was quite powerless. He could persuade Anna to return to town, but that would make her no safer than she was at Tolnitz, and she should be at Tolnitz until after the hastily arranged funeral. She was among friends there, and she would know better than he what to do in an emergency.

She had promised to telephone him at the office at nine o'clock. That was logical; a call from secretary to employer.

He knew his best course would be to wait till that call came through, but Babette's visit had worried him badly. He went downstairs and out by the back way. He walked through the streets till he was sure his shadow had not picked him up. Then he looked for a taxi.

When he said he wanted to go to Tolnitz, the driver objected. Without a police authorisation, no one could travel beyond the city limits. Check points had been established on all the roads into the country, and the occupants of all vehicles were being examined and turned back. No one had a chance of passing the police, not even a pedestrian. There were sentries along the Yalinsky Canal and all the river bridges were guarded. When Burton showed his press permit, the driver shrugged. "That will not to do to pass the cordon. But perhaps they will give you an authorisation at headquarters," he suggested. "Shall I drive you there?"

Burton shook his head. It would not be wise to advertise his intention to Sesnik. His previous visit to Tolnitz could be reasonably explained, but to show too much concern for Anna Maras might aggravate suspicion. He decided to wait for Anna's telephone call, and was back at the office a half hour before it was due. Wenzl was at his desk reading a book by Joseph Conrad. "Nothing has come in since eight, sir," he said. "Everything is on your desk."

Burton turned over the typewritten sheets. The Supreme Council would assemble at eleven in the morning. It was expected that the name of the new President would be given to the world at noon.

At five minutes to nine Burton sent Wenzl to the censor with a press message. "You needn't come back," he said. "If anything else turns up, I'll deal with it."

The telephone was silent. Burton paced the floor of the outer office, watching the instrument. He gave Anna another ten minutes, increased it to twenty. At nine-thirty he was still waiting in deepening anxiety. A minute later the bell rang and he leapt for the receiver.

It was Attridge with some fool question about the constitution of the Supreme Council.

"Sorry," said Burton curtly, "I'm waiting for an urgent call."

"Hold your horses a minute. I just want . . ."

"Sorry!"

He slammed down the receiver. He was trembling, and that was something that hadn't happened to him for a long time. He paced again in agitation. Footsteps sounded in the corridor and an agency message was pushed through the letter slot. He picked it up and read it without understanding a word. More footsteps, and the door was opened. A young man with his trouser ends clipped for cycling came into the room. He seemed to know Burton. He nodded and murmured a good evening, then held out a sealed envelope.

"This is for you," he said. "Forgive me, but I must not stay." Burton saw the handwriting and took the envelope eagerly. "One moment!"

The young man shook his head. "I can take no answer. I am not going back. It is easy enough to get into the city. Now I am here, I must remain."

Burton was reading the letter. When he looked up the messenger was gone. He read the letter again, more carefully:

It is impossible to telephone. Today I have had visitors and two of them are still here. They have searched the whole house and all papers have been taken away. It is plain that the place is to be kept under guard, but I do not expect they will interfere with my arrangements, as they will find nothing of interest in the papers. Sesnik has himself given sanction for the funeral, and I should be able to reach you early tomorrow evening as planned. If I should fail, you will know that you have my love.

Anna.

# XXIX

He had the assurance that she was still safe. He held to it through a restless night, but in the morning it seemed quite empty. Again he debated with himself whether or not he should attempt to go to her. He had a legitimate reason for applying for a travel authorisation to Tolnitz. He could say to Sesnik that he wished to be present at the burial of Anton Maras. Yet he had agreed with Anna that it would be best if he stayed away. It was important that he should be seen with her as little as possible and then only as her employer. She had urged this strongly, arguing that if he seemed too solicitous for her, he would later be suspected of having connived at her flight. Now that the escape plan was in suspense, if not entirely abandoned, the argument seemed less pressing. Yet he still hesitated. Settembrini was a man of resource. He might, in some way, get round the Ranawitz difficulty. The morning glittered with bright winter sunshine, but the city was tense and unresponsive beneath it. The interminable queue shuffled and inched towards the bier of President Riecke, and heads turned to watch the arrival of members of the Supreme Council at the House of Assembly on the other side of the great Square of the Parliament.

Burton and other foreign correspondents formed a small group on one side. Settembrini was on the steps below the colonnade, busy with his camera. Perhaps it was because he was such a good photographer that he was a privileged person on these occasions. The great and would-be great were susceptible to photographic flattery and Settembrini missed no opportunity of exploiting the fact. He was particularly active today, buttonholing his subjects after the click of the shutter, talking earnestly, gesticulating widely. Burton watched him, admiring the colossal impudence of the man. One potent signor of the co-operatives might administer a snub. Settembrini was ready for the next, unabashed. When the last member of the council had entered and the proceedings were due to start, he approached Burton.

"I have done my best," he said. "It is now in the lap of the gods."

Burton stared at him with fresh admiration.

"I told them all that the Ranawitz cancellation was a mistake," Settembrini added. "Some of them agreed with me. You will take this for what it is worth. If the decision goes to Halvic, we are beaten. If Varlein wins, we still have a chance. It may be a faint one, but, in the event, you will know what to do. I may not see you again. I shall be very busy. Karazelos will be in charge. He is a fool and a scoundrel but he will be reliable in this job ... if it comes off."

The little hope that this dogged refusal to accept defeat could kindle died in Burton before the deliberations had gone on for an hour. The meeting was in closest privacy. The news-paper men waited in the pressroom, two corridors away from the council chamber. It was to be a short meeting; everybody predicted that. Noon was the designated hour for the announcement, but at noon no announcement came. The deliberations went on, and there were rumours of dissension. One man who had contrived to get near the door of the chamber had heard voices raised in anger. The dragging on of time seemed to confirm the story. There was discord. The factions of Varlein and Halvic were locked in a struggle. One o'clock saw no end to it. At two the meeting adjourned until four. The disputants came out grimly from the chamber, the weight of the world upon their shoulders. They had nothing to say to the newspaper men. On the steps outside they waved Settembrini and his camera away.

Back in the office Wenzl was making progress with Joseph Conrad. He handed Burton a manila envelope with something bulky inside.

"This came for you a few minutes ago," he said.

The envelope bore the imprint of the State Tourist Bureau. It contained a scrawled note and a black rosette. The rosette had a red centre in the form of a scalloped rectangle with the name Ranawitz printed on it in black. The note said:

> This is to be worn by your nominee if the nine-o'clock train is restored. Z.K.

There was always that "if," yet it seemed that the final preparations were being made. Burton locked the rosette away in a drawer of his desk, glanced over the agency messages, then walked across to the Metropole to get something to eat.

When he returned to the House of the Parliament, the council was back at its deliberations. Attridge had started a game of pinochle and wanted him to join in. Burton declined. He stood by the window, looking out across the square at the patient line of people moving towards the hall where President Riecke rested. He wondered why he had come back to the pressroom, why he waited, hanging on a name. The agency flash would go out before he could get a cable to the censor, and it didn't matter much anyway. Yet the old instinct held him. This was news in the making. In New York they might shove it away somewhere on a middle page, but here it was news. He had to be in at the kill.

He turned from the window, impatient with himself. He had wasted too much of his life on this sort of thing. He wanted to get out of it. Only Anna Maras mattered. The rest was childish, as meaningless as the excitement of Attridge over a run and a roundhouse. Or this waiting for a name.

Attridge was dealing. He had good deft hands and the cards fell from them quickly. He picked up his hand, but before he could sort it, the door opened and one of the clerks of the council, a thin, elderly man, stood on the threshold.

This was it. The game of pinochle was over. The clerk cleared his throat with a thin noise.

"Gentlemen," he said, "the Supreme Council has ended its session, having considered a successor to President Riecke. I have the honour to announce that the name to be given to the people is that of Konstantin Varlein. There will be no more, gentlemen."

For Burton there was more. There was an echo of Settembrini: "If Varlein wins, we still have a chance."

The news was issuing from the loud-speakers in the streets as he handed in his cable. The honours and achievements of the President-designate poured from the wireless set as he entered the office. Wenzl moved to switch off.

"Leave it on," Burton told him. "Listen to all the bulletins and give me a translation of anything new. That's your job for the rest of the day."

The hoped-for announcement came in the six-thirty news. In these sad days of national grief over the passing of a be-loved figure, the new President felt that there was a double significance in the traditional ceremony at Ranawitz. At his express wish, the order cancelling the pilgrimage had been revoked. The arrangements previously announced would be carried out, and the opportunity would be taken to pay a special tribute to President Riecke, whose noble work as a leader of the Resistance was inspired by the martyrs of Ranawitz.

Burton took a wad of bank notes from his desk and made a call on Settembrini. The business completed, he hurried back to the office, hoping that Anna would have arrived. Wenzl was still listening dutifully to the radio. But he was alone. Anna was late. Burton stood at the window looking down at the street as if he hoped to pick her out from among the pedestrians. He was confident now that all would be well, but anxiety returned as the hour advanced. Someone was still talking over the air, and the sound from the outer office suddenly increased in volume. He wheeled to see if the door had been opened. She was there. She closed the door, shutting out the sound. She was weary after the ordeal of the day and the signs of grief were in her face. He moved to meet her, and held her tightly.

# XXX

Zeno Karazelos, wearing the badge of the State Tourist Bureau, bustled about as if he were the sole owner of the Alexis Station. It seemed that he wanted to help all who were travelling to Ranawitz by the nine-o'clock train and not merely those people who were distinguished by the black rosette with the scalloped rectangle in red.

"The rear coaches, please," he cried to hesitant mourners. "Plenty of room in the rear coaches. Plenty of room in the rear." For the red rectangle he had different advice, delivered more confidentially. "You will take the coach next to the engine. Do you understand? No other coach will do. The one next to the engine."

He saluted Burton with a finger to cap.

"This is Miss Maras, yes? Very well. I will look after her good. You have no fear."

It occurred to Burton that the Greek was expecting a tip.

"I'll see you on the train," he said. "I'm going as far as Ranawitz."

This simple statement seemed to confound the guide.

"Not in the same coach," he suggested secretively. "I have to keep the special party together."

"There's surely room enough," Burton answered.

Karazelos frowned. "Permit me to know what is best from the professional standpoint of organisation."

"I am travelling with Miss Maras as far as Ranawitz."

"Okay. I will fix it." Karazelos still didn't like the situation, but stood aside from the door of the coach. "You will find places in the first compartment." He left them abruptly to head off a family group. "The other coaches, please," he barked at them. "Plenty of room in the other coaches. This one is reserved."

The manner of it was blatant enough to make Burton shiver. If a station official became suspicious, Settembrini's plan might be jeopardised, but Karazelos seemed to have no thought of this, or he was confident that he would get away with it. He got away with it till the rest of the train was full. Then, when he was challenged by an aggressive ticket holder, he yielded. He had assembled his party in the one coach and there were many seats left over for others.

Five minutes to go, and Burton and Anna were still the only occupants of the first compartment. Karazelos joined them and stood in the doorway. Now that he could no longer defend the coach, he was determined to make a last ditch of the compartment. The latecomers filed past him along the corridor.

"Fools!" Karazelos exclaimed, and went on cryptically, "On their own heads be it! On their own heads!"

"What is going to happen?" said Anna.

"No questions please, madame."

Nine o'clock. The train still stood at the platform, but there were no more passengers to board it. The Greek looked at his watch twice in less than a minute.

"What's the matter now?" he muttered in English. "Why don't they start?"

Burton, too, was nervous, but suffered it silently. Anna sat in the corner facing the engine, leaning back, with a pallor of weariness in her face. The strain of the days and the sleepless nights had brought her to the point of exhaustion, yet there was still this tension to be borne, this waiting for the train to start.

At last came the warning cry, the thin, comical toot of the guard's horn, the shrill staccato note of the whistle, and the train lurched, shuddered, rattled its couplings, and moved forward.

Burton felt Anna's hand grip his and he returned the pressure. Karazelos closed the compartment door and, sinking down on the seat, let out a gasp of relief.

The train rolled, picked its way through the maze of tracks and switches, gathered speed along the riverbank, crossed the Garetsin Bridge, and roared through the suburbs.

Karazelos straightened himself up and was all assurance again. "You will understand, Mr. Burton, that you are now under my direction," he said. "I am responsible for the party and all the arrangements for their tour. You may stay with your friend till the check point is reached at Yakovin, two miles this side of Ranawitz. At Yakovin I will instruct you. I am warning you now because there must be no interference with my plans. I must ask you not to leave your seat till . . ."

The words ceased abruptly as the sliding door of the compartment was jerked open noisily. Karazelos shot into the corridor to resist the interloper.

"It is not permitted to enter. It is reserved. Official use only."

"Out of the way!" The retort came in a commanding snarl. "There are no reservations on this train. Get out of the way!"

Burton became rigid. The grip of Anna's hand on his was convulsive. The voice from the corridor was the voice of Sesnik.

# XXXI

The podgy figure in funereal black filled the narrow doorway as Karazelos swung back against the seat. The small eyes squinted from the moonlike face; the comical mouth had a grim set.

"My dear Anna! And Mr. Burton!" Sesnik spoke in English. "It is always most pleasant to see you, however mournful the circumstances of our meeting. I had no idea that you would be travelling on this train."

He waddled past the white-faced Karazelos, then spoke to him without turning his head. "Find another place for yourself! I wish to talk privately to my friends. March!"

Karazelos marched.

"Who is that interfering fool?" Sesnik demanded.

"I don't know." Over the first shock, Burton began to think quickly. "I never saw him before. No doubt he means well enough."

"Someone from the Tourist Bureau. Just typical of that inefficient clique of bureaucrats. They're always assuming authority where they have none. Forgive me. I do not like this sort of thing. What has the Tourist Bureau to do with this train? They are not running conducted tours to Ranawitz."

"I wouldn't know," said Burton.

Sesnik went into the corridor, glanced down the length of it, came back, closed the door, and turned to Anna.

"My dear, I don't think you should be making this trip. After the terrible bereavement you have suffered, you should have been allowed to rest for a few days." He shook his head sadly. "I am surprised, Burton, that you require her to return to work so soon."

"He did not require it," the girl protested.

"I see." The bassoon voice was gentle. "You prefer to have something to do. That is understandable, Anna, but you must not overtax yourself."

Burton stared through the window. The train was crossing the flat arable plains in the great loop of the Dreva to the north of the city.

"I deeply regret that I was unable to be at Tolnitz yesterday," Sesnik went on. "I hope that you received my message."

"Yes." Anna leaned back, closing her eyes.

"I had always the highest esteem for your dear father. I was shocked to learn of his sudden death. I know he was a sick man, but I was not prepared for the news. It has been a sad week indeed. First our distinguished President, then our great scholar and historian. A strange coincidence that they should be linked in death, as well as in life. I suppose Dr. Maras was deeply affected by the assassination?"

Anna remained silent, her eyes still closed.

Burton said, "Miss Maras is deeply affected by what she has been through. Don't you think you might let her alone for a few days?"

"My dear fellow!" Sesnik was pained. "I am merely trying to express my profound sympathy for her in her loss." "Do you have to do it in the form of a police interrogation?"

Anna sat up quickly. "I am quite all right," she said.

It was a plea for discretion and Burton knew it, but he doubted if discretion would lull Sesnik's suspicions. The reverse might well be true.

"I suppose you were expressing sympathy when you sent your men to Tolnitz to search the house?" he snapped. "And no doubt it was respect for Dr. Maras that led you to seize all his papers."

Sesnik shook his head sadly. "You must believe me, my dear Burton. These were things quite beyond my control. The orders came from a higher level. There was naturally a great interest in the circumstances of such a sudden death."

"So much so that you had to drag Anna in for questioning even before the event!"

"That was an error perpetrated by my colleague Gröte. I was away at the time. Gröte was influenced by the connection between your office and the criminal Trovic. His action was, perhaps, excusable. Nevertheless, he has been reprimanded."

"Is it the connection between my office and Trovic that causes you to travel on this train?"

Sesnik smiled. "You are so suspicious, Burton, I sometimes think you would have done well in my calling. I suppose you think I have had you followed again. Nothing I can say, of course, will disabuse you. What I cannot understand is why you imagine I should personally escort you on a newspaper mission to Ranawitz."

Zeno Karazelos, passing along the corridor, lurched against the compartment door as the motion of the train threw him off balance. He made a grimace which may have been a signal or merely a reaction to the bump.

Sesnik, slewed half round in the comer seat, observed nothing. He paused merely to take a breath, then went on. "No, my dear fellow. The truth of the matter is simple. I am on this train because extra police precautions are being taken at Ranawitz, and I wish to reach the place at the earliest possible moment to assure myself that orders have been carried out. As you know, Ranawitz is a mere two miles from the frontier, and . . . Well, I regret to say that we have had information that there is to be an escape attempt."

Anna's shoulder pressed against Burton's arm. It might have been the swaying of the train. He glanced at Sesnik and shrugged. "What's the use of telling me that? The censor wouldn't pass it."

"No, no. Of course not. It is strictly confidential." Sesnik shuffled his small polished shoes on the floor. "Off the record, as you put it. The scheme of these political criminals is to get to Ranawitz in the guise of peaceful pilgrims and then attempt the frontier at one or more points. We were afraid some of the Trovic gang might be among them, so we advised the cancellation of the ceremonies. But, late yesterday, as you know yourself, the order was revoked. So here we are, and I am pleased. The cancellation was not my idea. I am with President Varlein. He sees, as I do, that we have the criminals in a trap. What could be better than to lure them to Ranawitz? All we have to do is throw a cordon round the place and screen everybody. It will be as easy as netting fish, don't you think?"

"Sure, sure. Quite a trick." Burton stared out of the window. The train was beginning the long climb into the hills.

Karazelos passed the door again, followed this time by a train official. They were going in the direction of the second coach.

Anna rose from her seat. "I'm sorry," she said. "I must get a drink of water."

"I'll get it for you," Burton said.

She had given him the opening he needed in order to warn Karazelos, but, for a moment, he was afraid that she had made it too obvious. But Sesnik was quite unsuspicious. Or he was paying out rope. You never could tell.

"There is a special filter at this end of the coach," he said waving a fat hand. "With paper cups. We followed the American design. We like to be up-to-date in our railways. Next summer we shall have air-conditioned cars."

Burton hurried to the end of the coach. Corridor and toilet were empty. Karazelos and the guard had passed into the next coach. Burton tried the door. It was locked. If the Greek had arranged that, then he had cut himself off.

The filter was dry. Burton went back to the compartment.

"I'm sorry," he said. "No water. I couldn't get through to the next coach."

"The railway people are not always conscientious," Sesnik murmured.

"It does not matter," Anna said.

Sesnik looked at his watch. "We shall soon be at Yakovin. We stop there for a minute or two. The militia board the train to check tickets and papers. This is, of course, the normal precaution. The special screening will not begin till we have all the suspects at Ranawitz. You will find water at Yakovin."

At Yakovin, Burton thought, he might be able to get through to the rest of the train and warn Karazelos, though the warning might be of little use.

Sesnik's voice droned on. "Of course, for all we know, this very coach may be packed with the desperate criminals we are seeking . . . that impudent fellow who was in this compartment, for instance . . . but I assure you, we shall have the handcuffs on them before the day is out. . . ."

The engine panted loudly, hauling its load through a long cutting. Then there was a level stretch with hills crowding the track on either side, and, at last, Yakovin.

A warning whistle, and the train slowed down for the halt. The militia were waiting on the platform; eight or ten booted and belted lads with pistols in their holsters.

Burton was on the platform as soon as the train stopped. Yakovin consisted of a rain shelter, a small wooden shed, and a signal box, but Burton gave scarcely a glance to the local scenery. He saw Karazelos running forward from the third coach, followed by the guard. He saw a tap and filled a paper cup in case Sesnik was watching. When he turned from the tap, the guard was doing something to the couplings between the first and second coaches. Several militiamen had boarded the train. Two more were dashing towards the engine. Everybody seemed to be in a desperate hurry, as if there were not a second to spare. Burton caught the Greek by the sleeve. Karazelos got in the first word.

"I told you not to move," he hissed. "Do you want to spoil everything?"

"Everything is spoiled," Burton told him. "Sesnik knows the whole plan."

"Sesnik knows nothing. He is a fool. Get into the second coach at once. I was coming to instruct you. You must not go back to the girl."

"I'm going back. You can't do anything now. You'd better warn your people. I'll look after Anna Maras."

Karazelos clutched his head and swore bitterly. "Must there always be this amateur interference?" he demanded. "This is the point where I take over. I am directing you to the second coach. It is important. Get on board at once."

Sesnik appeared. "What is the trouble?" he asked. "Is this imbecile interfering again?" He shouted something at the Greek.

Karazelos fell back, muttering. Burton climbed back to his coach, holding his cup of water. "It's all right," he told Sesnik. "I was asking the man if it was potable. Perhaps he didn't understand me." The whistle sounded a warning blast. There was movement again. A lurch, a pull. Karazelos scrambled on board and slammed the door. All the militiamen seemed to be in the first coach. The corridor was full of them. Anna took the cup of water and drank it. Karazelos glared sulkily in through the glass panel of the compartment door. The train developed speed till it swayed and rattled alarmingly.

Burton looked through the window and saw the moving shadow at the side of the permanent way. He blinked his eyes and looked again, then nudged Anna. The racing shadow was of an engine and one coach. There was nothing else. The rest of the train had been left behind at Yakovin. That guard fumbling with the couplings . . .

Sesnik twisted in his seat. "The driver must be mad," he

exclaimed. "There will be an accident in a moment."

Faster, and faster. Then a glimpse of a bleak collection of weather-toned ruins and people moving among them. A flash, the flick of a camera shutter. Ranawitz.

Sesnik saw it. He pulled his bulky body up from the seat, but was thrown back again by the rocking and swaying of the coach. He pulled himself up a second time, gasping. His moonface was blotched with anger, his small eyes burned. "Ranawitz!" he gasped. "Ranawitz! Stop the train! Stop!" He reached for the emergency lever with his fat hand. At that moment Karazelos rolled back the door and poked him in the waistcoat with the muzzle of a Luger.

"Sit down!" Karazelos commanded, and a lurch of the careering coach sent Sesnik sprawling. The Greek took the opposite seat. In the corridor the militiamen were grinning, but they grinned with their hands on their pistols.

Sesnik's bassoon became a shrill oboe. "Arrest that man!" he screamed, pointing at Karazelos. "Arrest him!"

The false militiamen laughed out loud. Karazelos moved his Luger menacingly. "I told you," he said, "that this compartment was reserved. You insisted on riding with us. It is too late for you to change your mind." He turned to Burton. "You, too, my friend, were warned. You were to have been spared this trip, but you would not listen. I don't know what the consequences will be for you, but I take no responsibility. I have enough to do to look after the passengers who have paid their fares."

"Stop the train!" Sesnik screamed again. "We'll all be killed."

"You'd better settle down to it, Sesnik," Burton advised him. "I wanted to get off at Ranawitz too, but I don't mind going on. It suits me fine."

"Going on? Where are we going?"

Karazelos answered. "Across the frontier. Into the American zone."

"You're mad!" Sesnik turned frantically to Burton. "We're in the hands of a criminal lunatic. The frontier guard has orders to shoot.

The viaduct is mined. We'll all be blown up."

"What will your guards shoot at?" the Greek demanded. "Will they blow up a good viaduct to stop a runaway engine with one coach? We'll be across the viaduct before they can pull a switch. They won't even see us till we're out of the tunnel."

"Madman! Murderer!" Sesnik tried to rise, but was promptly thrust back. There was commotion in the corridor. The unwilling passengers were causing trouble. A shot was fired. Women started to scream.

"You knew of this, Burton!" Sesnik gasped. "You've joined in it to help that girl. You'll both go back as prisoners, and your paper won't be able to help you. You'll all go back as prisoners. All of you!"

Burton ignored him. He held Anna close, his arm round her. "Don't worry," he told her. "I'll be with you all the time now." The time might be very brief. The engine and coach clattered and roared into a tunnel—the tunnel. The noise stayed the commotion in the other compartments. There was no more screaming. The grim silence of waiting was wrapped in the din of the dark passage. The locomotive might have been plunging into the pit. Minutes, interminable minutes. Then they flashed into the glare of day again and were on the curving viaduct, the last span before the frontier post.

Those who could crowd to the windows saw the uniformed guards running frantically on the other side of the gorge. They saw the long painted beam of the wooden barrier across the rails at the actual border line. It seemed to rush towards them as they watched, and then they were warned against watching.

"Down, everybody!" Karazelos shouted, and the cry was taken up along the corridor.

Sesnik sat doggedly in his corner, defying fate. Others complied with the order, and they were just in time. Bullets shattered the glass of the windows and thudded into the woodwork. The patter of metal against the steel sheath of the coach was like hail on a tin roof.

Then, subduing everything else, came the giant roar of a mine. The coach lurched drunkenly but sped on behind its engine. A crash. The beam was shattered and the train was through, rushing on down a long cutting, along the road to freedom.

# XXXII

They were all under arrest. The young lieutenant at the frontier post was not quite sure what to do.. He asked for instructions from area headquarters, and the area officer found it necessary to get in touch with a higher command. Nothing like this had happened before. The young lieutenant became rather tired of explaining it all to one after another of his superiors. "Yes, sir, a train. That's to say, a locomotive and day coach. Dashed across the viaduct and crashed the gate. The Reds opened fire, then exploded a mine this side of the viaduct. A section of the track was ripped up, but just too late to stop the train. Two of the passengers were hit by bullets, not seriously. . . . Did you say how many bullets? . . . Oh, passengers! Sixty-eight in all. Thirty-seven of them are claiming asylum. One of them says he's Charles Burton of the New York *Star-Dispatch*. . . . Yes. He's alongside me now. Wants to get through to his Vienna office with his secretary. . . . Very well, sir. I'll wait."

Zeno Karazelos was slightly drunk and very talkative. "It was easy. I am a great organiser. We seized the check point at Yakovin ten minutes before the train was due. We had these men disguised in militia uniforms and another was on the train with me, dressed as a railway guard. The real militia were overpowered and locked up with the station staff. When the engine pulled up, our guard uncoupled the coach from the rest of the train while two of our militia knocked out the driver and fireman. One of them knew all about locomotives. He was our key man. The telephone and telegraph lines had been cut, so when we started again the frontier could not be warned. It was easy. I am undoubtedly clever."

Senior officers arrived, examined the bullet-riddled coach, and started to question the prisoners. Karazelos had his party lined up and drawn apart from the bewildered and frightened group of the forcibly abducted. Burton and Anna waited with Karazelos. Sesnik would have nothing to do with any of them. He had stormed and protested and complained, demanding that the whole coach load should be sent back across the frontier in his charge. "I place them all under arrest," he shouted. "They are traitors, criminals, assassins. They are in my custody." "You're out of your territory," the lieutenant had told him. "They're in my custody, and that goes for you, too."

"I wish to make a formal complaint. I demand that you get in immediate communication with the representative of my country in Vienna."

"You'll have to wait till the colonel comes."

The colonel had come, but now Sesnik was less sure of himself. He stood in isolation, a dejected figure. The colonel dealt with the others first; those who wanted protection and those who wished to be sent back. At last it was Sesnik's turn, and, for some reason, his anger had evaporated; the bassoon was dulcet, almost ingratiating.

"Well?" the colonel asked. "What do you wish to do?"

Sesnik teetered on his shining shoes. "Now that I am here," he answered, "I will stay. I wish to be treated as a political refugee." Suddenly his jaw dropped and a look of pure astonishment spread over his face. "In fact," he added in wonderment, "I am a political refugee!"

Karazelos was annoyed. Did they think Settembrini was a philanthropist, running people across the frontier free of charge? It wasn't right.

"I should let Settembrini worry about that," said Burton. "What's it matter to you, anyway?"

Karazelos shrugged in disgust and turned away. "It isn't business," he muttered; but he muttered in Greek, and neither Burton nor Anna Maras heard him.

They were free.

# Eric Ambler

## Doctor Frigo

ISBN: 978-07551-1761-1

A coup d'etat in a Caribbean state causes a political storm in the region and even the seemingly impassive and impersonal Doctor Castillo, nicknamed Doctor Frigo, cannot escape the consequences. As things heat up, Frigo finds that both his profession and life are horribly at risk.

*'As subtle, clever and complex as always'* - Sunday Telegraph
*'The book is a triumph'* - Sunday Times

## Judgment on Deltchev

ISBN: 978-07551-1762-8

Foster is hired to cover the trial of Deltchev, who is accused of treason for allegedly being a member of the sinister and secretive Brotherhood and preparing a plot to assassinate the head of state whilst President of the Agrarian Socialist Party and member of the Provisional Government. It is assumed to be a show trial, but when Foster encounters Madame Deltchev the plot thickens, with his and other lives in danger ....

*'The maestro is back again, with all his sinister magic intact'* - The New York Times

## The Levanter

ISBN: 978-07551-1763-5

Michael Howell lives the good life in Syria, just three years after the six day war. He has several highly profitable business interests and an Italian office manager who is also his mistress. However, the discovery that his factories are being used as a base by the Palestine Action Force changes everything - he is in extreme danger with nowhere to run ...

*'The foremost thriller writer of our time'* - Sunday Times
*'Our greatest thriller writer'* - Graham Greene

# ERIC AMBLER

## The Schirmer Inheritance

ISBN: 978-07551-1765-9

Former bomber pilot George Carey becomes a lawyer and his first job with a Philadelphia firm looks tedious - he is asked to read through a large quantity of files to ensure nothing has been missed in an inheritance case where there is no traceable heir. His discoveries, however, lead to unforeseen adventures and real danger in post war Greece.

*'Ambler towers over most of his newer imitators'* - Los Angeles Times
*'Ambler may well be the best writer of suspense stories .. He is the master craftsman'* - Life

## Topkapi (The Light of Day)

ISBN: 978-07551-1768-0

Arthur Simpson is a petty thief who is discovered stealing from a hotel room. His victim, however, turns out to be a criminal in a league well above his own and Simpson is blackmailed into smuggling arms into Turkey for use in a major jewel robbery. The Turkish police, however, discover the arms and he is further 'blackmailed' by them into spying on the 'gang' - or must rot in a Turkish jail. However, agreeing to help brings even greater danger ....

*'Ambler is incapable of writing a dull paragraph'* - The Sunday Times

# Eric Ambler

## Siege at the Villa Lipp (Send No More Roses)

ISBN: 978-07551-1766-6

Professor Krom believes Paul Firman, alias Oberholzer, is one of those criminals who keep a low profile and are just too clever to get caught. Firman, rich and somewhat shady, agrees to be interviewed in his villa on the French Riviera. But events take an unexpected turn and perhaps there is even someone else artfully hiding in the deep background?

*'One of Ambler's most ambitious and best'* - The Observer
*'Ambler has done it again ... deliciously plausible'* - The Guardian

## Tender to Danger (Tender to Moonlight)

ISBN: 978-07551-1767-3

*(Ambler originally writing as Eliot Reed with Charles Rodda)*

A blanket of fog grounds a flight in Brussels and Dr. Andrew Maclaren finds himself sharing a room with a fellow passenger who by morning disappears in suspicious circumstances, leaving behind an envelope hidden under the carpet. Whilst the contents are seemingly innocent, they lead the young Doctor into nightmarish adventures, culminating in the avoidance of cold-blooded killers in a deserted windmill and in the company of a beautiful redhead.

Made in the USA
Coppell, TX
15 October 2021